I0598301

The SAFE PLACE

BRANDON M. ROGERS

LUCIDBOOKS

The Safe Place

Copyright © 2025 by Brandon M. Rogers

Published by Lucid Books in Houston, TX
www.LucidBooks.com

All rights reserved. No part of this publication may be reproduced, stored in a retrieval system, or transmitted in any form by any means, electronic, mechanical, photocopy, recording, or otherwise, without the prior permission of the publisher, except as provided for by USA copyright law.

ISBN: 978-1-63296-878-4 (Paperback)
ISBN: 978-1-63296-879-1 (Hardback)
eISBN: 978-1-63296-880-7

Special Sales: Most Lucid Books titles are available in special quantity discounts. Custom imprinting or excerpting can also be done to fit special needs. Contact Lucid Books at Info@LucidBooks.com

For my grandmother, Mary Tucker Anderson (1937–2022), who stood in the gap for me every day of my life and showed me the true meaning of faith in action.

And for my wife, whose superpower is the ability to see straight into the heart of others, enabling us to grow together as one.

TABLE OF CONTENTS

SPECIAL THANKS

I want to thank Mike Mahoney for his unwavering guidance and support. Marlene Backert, your inspiration sparked the very idea for this book. To all the families who opened their homes and hearts to me—your generosity means more than words can express.

Thank you to my entire family for being a constant source of inspiration. To my aunt, for offering a heart full of wisdom and guidance without judgment. To the Quinns, Shue's, and Ferrigno's, for giving me a home inside and outside of my heart.

I owe much to my friends, whose encouragement helped me finally complete this book. A special thank you to Jeremy, Andrew, Chris, Dan, Tiff, Justin, Chad, Michelle, Layne, Sean, Bentley, Pat, Tony, Brian, whose friendship and insight have been instrumental in the development of this story.

To Laura, your force and inspiration were critical in bringing this work to completion. And to Bailee and Henlee—without you, I wouldn't have found the drive to finish this book and keep dreaming.

Lastly, I thank God for the care and purpose in every moment of the last 44 years. I am forever grateful.

Chapter 1

CITY LOVE

He was both angry and ashamed. He'd been married for all of 6 months and already the habits of old began creeping back into his daily routine. How pathetic. He had married the love of his life and left behind the man he'd become. That's what he told himself the day he got married.

The drugs, the constant pursuit of attention, the insurmountable need to be heard and recognized... it was all in the past. At least, that was his intention.

There weren't many options for him at this point. The ultimatum she gave didn't leave much in the way of ambiguity. Jocelyn was either going to leave him, or he was going to concede and get some professional help. After years of chasing her affection, he had finally drawn her into the dysfunction of his world. It should be noted that she did so willingly and fully aware of the baggage he was toting along. Despite it all, she was fed up. So, he got in the car and began to drive.

The counseling appointment wasn't too far from his house, but he wanted time to get there a bit earlier just in case he had some sort *of revelation that might get him out of this mess. All he could do was think about whether or not she would still be in their apartment when he came back. He did not feel sorry for himself in the least. This was, after all, his fault.*

He gripped the steering wheel a little tighter than usual, feeling the slickness of his own palm against the leather. The hum of the tires on the asphalt seemed louder than the radio. Somewhere under the shame and the anxiety, a quieter thought began to stir: this couldn't be the whole story. He didn't know what came next, but some part of him sensed that the road he was on – the night, this appointment – was going to decide if he ever truly came home to himself.

September – 2006

An alarm sounded. It was two minutes before seven on a Friday morning. The delivery trucks consumed the streets of the big city, talking to one another in high-pitched frequencies. Never mind them… his headache was the only thing he could think about. Well, that and the strange woman immediately to his left still asleep. He hadn't a clue who she was or where she came from. Fortunately for him, this wasn't his apartment. Which meant he could make an exit before any answers might be demanded revealing his utter lack of self-control. *What the hell happened last night,* he asked himself?

He began to gather himself and pieced together his wardrobe from the prior night. His clothes were strewn all over the apartment; a sock here and a shoe there. It was like a dysfunctional scavenger hunt. Before leaving, he glanced back at his new acquaintance wondering if she might wake up with the same unfamiliarity plaguing her. If such were the case, it might absolve him from any feelings of guilt. He was kidding himself and he knew it.

As he made his way to the door, he noticed a coffee table coated with some of what must have been the previous night's festivities. The fleeting "fix" in the form of a fine, white powder that was staring at him from that glass table might help mask his misguided moral compass, if even only for a moment. *Perhaps just one line to wake up and maybe alleviate this headache* he thought. One line down, and then a second quickly followed. His eyes perked wide open, and his heart began to beat with rapid vigor and intention. It was Friday. A quick workday and the weekend happy hour would be waiting to rescue him from the wear of the week. He closed the door with a gentle decency, as if the gesture was somehow a shadow of the gentleman he thought himself to be.

What a self-righteous prick.

The walk wasn't too bad... just a few blocks from his 5th floor, two-bedroom apartment in midtown. With each step, last night's hangover fog that blanketed his brain began to lift. He began thinking about the woman he'd just left. She wasn't a stranger. Thank God for that. Her name was Kristen, and they had met through a mutual friend over a work dinner a few months ago. As he paged through his cell phone's text history, it occurred to him that she was a late-night connection after hours of bar hopping with his colleagues. He wondered if every guy in their mid-twenties behaved this way. He then thought of his sisters, the way they revered the chivalrous demeanor with which he'd be raised, and what they might think of his current lifestyle had they been walking home with him on that particular morning. It was too early to indulge that rabbit hole. It was nearly 8 am.

His apartment was exceptionally clean and organized. The need for his mausoleum-type environment used to be a way for him to edge away his own anxiety. Now, it was just something to impress his visitors.

Classic narcissist.

Each time he walked through the doorway, without fail, he placed his keys to the right of the entrance on a small shelf with a few hooks and a wooden placard that read "*welcome home.*" The thought of changing the words to "*go home*" occasionally crossed his mind on nights when he felt exceptionally introspective. There he might find some redemption for the sorry excuse of a human being he'd turned into. It was too early for introspection. Instead, he threw his clothes in their respective "to be dry cleaned" and "to be laundered" bins and made his way to the shower.

He heard his phone ringing from the shower… undoubtedly his grandmother checking in as was her usual routine at this point in the morning. She was the only woman he loved or respected. He had closed himself off emotionally sometime around six years old and had since continued to move in that direction. Break-ups, abandonment, you know, the usual Freudian rationale to help comfort his choice in bad decisions. Regardless, he had not closed himself off to her. She was the reflection of any unconditional love that might exist in his world. And, at 25, he didn't need any other kind from any other person. Which was fine by him.

Conversations with "*The Gram*" were as predictable as much as they were necessary. Her inquiries were cyclical in nature. *Are you getting enough sleep* she would ask? *Are you taking care of your body and trusting God?* She was married to her religion. Ironically, she was a terrible sleeper and an incessant worrier. Maybe that's why she insisted on making sure he was taking care of himself. If only she knew the truth. If only he had the gumption to tell her.

He figured he'd call her during his morning stroll. The distance to the office was four blocks east and two blocks north, which afforded him fifteen minutes of conversation before stopping at the deli in the bottom floor of his office building to purchase an Orangina (a French, orange sparkling water) and imbibe two 30 milligram immediate release Adderall. He might shove down a quick two-egg and bacon bagel if time permitted. But that was on the bottom of his list of ingestible priorities. If he could find the time, it would help the amphetamines settle in his stomach a bit more easily. The ache on his empty stomach could last an hour or more… a small price to pay for the benefit it provided.

Right on cue, he called his Gram and was greeted by all the typical questions in her arsenal.

"Morning, sweetheart. Are you getting enough sleep, Tristan?"

He smiled at himself, though his eyes stung. "Morning, Gram. Yeah… I'm fine. Got plenty of sleep."

"Mmm. I can hear it in your voice. You're running too hard. Have you prayed today?"

He hesitated, watching a delivery truck splash through a pothole and was reluctant to layer a second lie in this short dialogue. "Of course I have. I'm good, Gram. Promise."

Clearly, he wasn't that reluctant.

"I know you're busy. I just… I love you, Tristan. But remember, God loves you more."

This always centered Tristan, even in the worst of states. He couldn't fathom how someone so perfect in her definition and delivery of love could be outdone by something greater. But she maintained that her faith and her God somehow made her inferior. Nevertheless, he acquiesced and told her exactly what she needed to hear… and exactly what he always wanted to genuinely mean. "I know, Gram. I love you, too."

On this particular phone call, she spent the majority of her time lecturing him (in the sweetest of ways) homing in on two specific topics: his sleep and his prayer life. He was less than equipped to handle such depth that early in his day. Despite two emphatic negative responses to her questions bouncing off the walls of his mind (never to actually be spoken aloud), he appeased her sense of responsibility for him and made it clear that both his sleep and his prayer life were in good order. It made him feel as though she wouldn't worry. At least, not more than her usual. She always ended each talk by reminding him that she loved him, but that God loved him more. She was 69 years old. No sense in arguing who loved whom.

Every day he took the elevator to the 12th floor, which always seemed to take forever considering the number of stops the thing made. The layout of his trading floor was typical for the industry. Rows of desks barely bigger than shoulder width were lined up and down like something you might see in a military training facility. His particular desk had four monitors, stacked two by two, and was partitioned only slightly by a six-inch divider on each side. Sufficed to say, privacy was at premium. And despite his salary, he was low man on the totem pole, which meant no privacy at all. That may have bothered him, looking like he had just been hit by a truck toting several kilos of Cocaine, except that his colleagues on both sides were also a party to his weekly debauchery. Last night was no exception.

A couple of hours had passed since his morning dose of Adderall. He glanced briefly at the clock as if the time would have mattered and took down two more pills. The milligram count was now at 120 and it was barely 10am. It wasn't that he was addicted. Scratch that, he was absolutely addicted. It was more because it elevated his capacity to move in and out of the countless tickers streaming on the screens just a foot in front of his face. He moved with more speed and motivation on the drugs. Coincidentally, they also served to mask the look on his face, which communicated just how truly worn he was. This "trader's script" was common among twenty-somethings on The Street. For him, however, it was gluttonous. Most needed it to get that added advantage. He already had that edge. It was a flagrant abuse of a gift he had taken for granted his entire life.

It wasn't always abused. He could remember when it first set in, early in his grammar school years. It was far from a gift at that stage. It was confusing and it was not something about which he ever spoke. Most kids touted themselves on how fast they could run on the playground, or how well they could make it from one end of the monkey bars to the other. Those gifts were typical gifts for normal children. All he wanted was to be normal. But this gift would never allow for such a life. While most kids were learning to read words and work on their pronunciation, all he could do was memorize them. No matter how much he tried, he would look at the words they would read as a class or at home as a family and he could, almost verbatim from the very beginning, recite the book without looking at a single page.

He had an eidetic memory. Most aren't even familiar with that word. It's quite rare for anyone older than 10. But, for the layman, it's referred to as a photographic memory. Words and numbers were like pictures pronounced with vivid articulation. And nothing was skewed or bent. They were stuck there as if they were created there, right in the center of his mind's eye. The interesting thing about it all was that for the first nine years of his life he spent his academic life in remedial classes. He was slow. It would be politically incorrect to call him *retarded*, but the thought crossed his parents minds more than once. Of course, he wasn't actually slow. This was just what his teachers saw. They couldn't comprehend that he was processing information internally and spent little time writing out his work or even verbally communicating his work. On the contrary, he was rather quiet. He didn't talk much. His IQ was tested in third grade and rated him at a 104. He was far from a genius. What did it all mean? Not a thing. It meant that he wasn't born with the gift masquerading as intelligence, and when it finally revealed itself to him, he wielded it like the emotional child that he was.

There was good reason for his behavior, however.

The high afforded him from the Adderall continued to coarse through his blood stream, elevating his mental and physical reflexes. He would occasionally look around at others who seemed to be moving with the same anxious speed he was. He could tell they were on some variation of his prescription, too. Odds were, however, that they didn't have a complimentary mental *gift* that he carried effortlessly.

Considering the inherent competitive advantage, he held over just about everyone he knew, the use of Adderall might have appeared a bit unnecessary. But no one knew just how his mind worked and how clearly it retained information. And on the infrequent occasion that he did slip up and talk about it (typically when he was high or drunk), it was regarded as bullshit, and he was quick to accommodate the notion. The knock to his ego was preferable to the attention he didn't want and the explanation he couldn't articulate.

It was just after 1pm and he had not eaten since breakfast. Unfortunately, the pills suppressed his appetite, so he would opt for another 60 milligrams of his favorite orange pill and press on with more of the numbers. The financial world was vast and both simple and complex. Derivative finance wasn't for the faint of heart. Very few financially-minded professionals had the ability to understand it, and even fewer had the ability to put it into practice. It required a capacity for thought that was very unique for his field. The morality of his work, on the other hand, was a whole other story. That, whether he knew it or not, was also weighing heavily on him.

He pushed through another two hours of number crunching before realizing, on that particular day, that he might need to work the weekend. He'd never get it done in the city. There would be entirely too much distraction if he stayed local. The only shot he'd have to meet his Monday deadline would be to take the last train down to his sister's just 130 short miles south of the city.

So, with that in mind, he popped three more Adderall (for those keeping count, he had now ingested 270 mgs – enough to keep a normal human brain awake for the better part of a week) and focused hard on his work. He continued to pour through portfolio after portfolio, working on adjusting each valuation based on the day's market movement. As his colleagues began to peel away for the weekend, he kept his head down. The train wouldn't be leaving for a couple more hours, which would be plenty of time to enjoy the cerebral high he'd been on for the majority of the day and pound out some additional work.

Finally, he looked up and saw that it was time to make his way to terminal. He didn't know it then, but it would be the last time he would take that train from that station in that city. Ever.

As he pulled into the church parking lot, he began to cry. This would become a recurring theme over the coming weeks. He couldn't help but belabor the events leading up to this moment. He understood that it was inevitable… dealing with all those decades of pain and dysfunction and abuse. He also knew just how much energy would be required of him to walk this road out.

He put the car in park and stared at the building wondering what was waiting for him on the other side of that entrance. At this point he was just exhausted. He thought about Paul's words from the book of Romans… "I do not do what I want, but I do the very thing I hate." He never really gave much thought to this as the words always felt commonsensical to him. The last fifteen years of his life had been spent doing the things he didn't want to do and not having the fortitude to always act on the things he knew were best for him.

He still had some time before his scheduled appointment. His eyes felt heavy and began to close as his thought process circled back to that last train ride from New York.

As was common during his trips back to see family, his mind almost involuntarily gave way to the overwhelming guilt of his city living. He knew he was walking in a body that no longer belonged to him. Emotionally he had stopped connecting... to anything or to anyone. He was beholden to the shiny carrots of materialism and self-serving desires of the flesh. He had no idea who he was.

Thankfully, he had a resolve for that, as well.

Each evening, following the rapid movement of his work, he would sip a glass of scotch accompanied by some Xanax to slow his artificial speed down a gear or two. Typically, he would take 4 or 5 milligrams to fall asleep. For some reason he disregarded his typical dose and doubled it. Maybe it was because he knew he needed a little more to offset the asinine amount of Adderall he'd consumed that day. But that would only be half true. The reality was that he was being picked up by his sister... someone for whom he had the deepest respect and couldn't allow her to see his state.

He walked to the back of the train car and slipped into the restroom. He changed out of his sweat-soaked business attire and threw on a t-shirt and a pair of jeans. He took five Xanax with some water and then crushed up the other four pills right there on the unsanitary bathroom sink. He then rolled up a $20 bill and snorted every bit of the white dust up his nose. This way, it would act more immediately, and he might have a chance at passing for normal when his sister greeted him.

The train was still about a half hour away from his stop when he began to feel an awkward shock-like feeling run down his right arm. It startled him at first, but he then realized that this was not an unfamiliar feeling. A few months back, during a concert at which he partook in an excessive amount of extracurriculars, he had the same feeling. It was as if his arm was beginning to lose feeling, and his mind started to glaze over with subtle tremors emerging every few seconds. This felt very similar to that night.

He allowed it to continue trying hard not to give it more attention than it needed. It was hard not to feel scared. He began to perspire again, essentially negating the whole purpose of changing just a few minutes prior. And then something happened. For the first time in his life, he lost vision for just a moment. It was like a bolt of lightning flew across his line of sight and all went white. Just then, the train stopped, and he heard his location called over the intercom.

His oldest sister stood waiting for him as his train pulled into the station just after 9 pm. As he stepped off the train, he experienced that same surge of light once more. Unfortunately for him, this time his sister was staring right at him and could see that something was wrong. She must have asked him a half a dozen times if he was ok, to which he would remark that he just needed to get back to her house and lay down. If only he had that much time.

They managed their way to her car... almost. Just before reaching for the door, he lost all feeling in his legs and collapsed. He couldn't remember much between the time he fell and the time he woke up, only the sound of some people gathering around and some harsh, bright lights flickering. When he did finally come to, he found himself strapped to a hospital bed, a tube lodged down his throat, an oxygen mask over his nose, and three doctors tending to him. He couldn't make out any words and continued to slip in and out of consciousness over those next few hours.

From a clinical perspective, Tristan lay there overdosing on that hospital bed surrounded only by the fear that it may be his last night alive.

Chapter 2

THE FIRE

He was tentative to leave his car. Despite having some negative preconceived notions based on past psychiatric evaluations, something told Tristan that this experience would prove different. Perhaps it was intuition; a gift to which he paid little to no attention. Still, a flutter deep in his heart he often confused with anxiety was prompting him to move. He hesitated. His will was stubborn and strong. He then began to spiral again down the rabbit hole of all the "what if" scenarios that might excuse him from the inevitability of this appointment. Or at least buy him a little time.

But it wasn't about him in this moment. It was about her. It was about the promise he made. It was about the ten years he had pinned over winning her heart and her love. If for no other reason, she was enough. She would always be enough. And if he was going to prove that to her, he would need to start by getting out of the car.

The parking lot was scarce. Thank God for that. He cared so much about people seeing him... what they might see or infer or, worse yet, tell others. The microscope under which he placed *himself felt intensely magnified. He typically wanted to be the center of attention. He needed that validation. Right now, however, he wanted none of that.*

So, he started to walk… slowly. Extremely slowly. Before he reached the door, he stopped and gave permission for his mind to take over. Anything that might stall the conversation that was awaiting him. His thoughts wandered back to the overdose Tristan endured just a few years before. His heart rate elevated. As he felt its beat quicken, he opened the door and retreated back to the driver's seat.

Tristan just sat there in his car recalling the events of his time in the Emergency Room. A barrage of imagery seemed as though it would continue through the sequence of events in that hospital, but then something changed. His mind quickly moved to the moment it all started. The moment when his life changed course. Suddenly, he was no longer strapped down to a bed covered with white sheets and fitted with metal handrails. Rather, he was thrown back into his childhood home.

And right there, in the center of his mind, was six-year old Tristan. What ensued would prove to be a significantly painful memory he had hoped was buried beyond the point of recollection. But, after nearly 20 years of repression forced out of sheer need for self-preservation, it was as if he was watching a video taken back in January of 1987. It was so clear that he felt paralyzed by the accuracy of the recall.

The first image was one of that six-year-old boy picking up a lighter. A red BIC lighter. He couldn't prepare his heart for the mental resurgence that would follow.

January – 1988

It was the January following his sixth birthday. It was late enough into the month that the decorations had been taken down and his winter break was over. The semester had started just a couple weeks prior and Tristan begrudged each day he was forced to go. He wasn't a fan of school... at least not first grade. Perhaps it was because nothing seemed to come as naturally as it did for other kids his age. He couldn't focus on anything for longer than a minute or two. He would just space out with no real reason as to why. He began noticing things about his behavior that seemed bizarre and often inconsistent with his siblings and peers. His incessant and sometimes involuntary daydreaming often carried him to places where he, himself, wore a cape and solved the woes of the world. Something about the thought of caring for others and being a hero appealed greatly to Tristan. They intrigued him and inspired him to keep dreaming. Inevitably, however, he would be aggressively interrupted by an angered teacher or his mother or father, frustrated that he had escaped whatever conversation in which he was supposed to be engaged. He just couldn't help it. He hated that he didn't fit.

Marie was different. She was Tristan's twin sister. She was normal. She was more than normal. She was so lovely and caring and protective. She was the half of the two of them that made them whole. Without her, Tristan was hardly even a half at all. Everyone loved Marie. And he loved that everyone loved her. After all, he was six and she was his protector. He hadn't yet understood the role of gender – nor did it bother him that she did most of the talking for the two of them. She was better at speaking, anyway. She was better at just about everything they did together. That was fine by him.

Her friends enjoyed her, and from his perspective, she didn't struggle with any weird thoughts. He probably could have asked her about the things that were running through his mind. They had their own language and their own code. He could say anything to her. But he felt scared at the notion.

"You ever wish we could just... not go to school today?" Tristan whispered, peeking out from under his blanket.

Marie grinned, twirling a strand of her hair as she so habitually caressed her thumb on the very same style blanket their Gram had crocheted for the two of them when they were born. "You mean every day?"

"Yeah, but just today. Just you and me. We could make peanut butter sandwiches and watch cartoons."

"Mom would find us. She always does." She said, rolling her eyes but leaning closer. "But maybe... one day."

Sadly, keeping things to himself is what got him in trouble. It's not that his intention was ever to cause trouble. That wasn't a motivation as much as a part of his makeup. Rather, his curiosity was the true culprit. There were lighters literally in every room of his house. His parents were walking cigarette commercials, constantly either lighting up or extinguishing a Marlboro or Virginia Slim. He would let his mind wander to a place where he would see those lighters ignite a flame that would require the help of superpowers. Perhaps the ability to freeze the fire. Maybe it was wind. To Tristan, it didn't matter. He just wanted to be the one to save everyone. And so, it wasn't abnormal, at least not to him, to find flames insatiably fascinating.

Every now and again, when no one was looking, he would grab one of the lighters and pretend he could control the flame. They were childproof, of course, which made it all but impossible for him to actually create an actual flame. Nevertheless, he would work hard to make it happen. After some serious practice, Tristan finally sparked his first flame. He was quite proud of himself. Getting it to work was pretty neat. Watching that flame dance just inches from his eyes was way more interesting, however.

And to think, the course of his life would all change with one flick of a lighter.

He wasn't a pyro or an arsonist. He didn't light fires to hurt or destroy. He was simply fascinated by their colors. Again, images and letters and numbers (at least at this point in his life) imprinted on his mind like an ink stamp with no way of washing off. Fire was beautiful and the colors were entrancing. He didn't understand what memory was or how it worked. He was just a boy with a vivid imagination, and that's all he was.

One mid-January morning he felt the need to stay home and pretend to be sick. It seems odd that a child his age would want to miss out on the opportunity to be with children his own age, but that's not what kept him back. In fact, that was the only thing that excited him about school. No, it was the monotony of spelling and adding and repetition that bored him and drove in him a sense of distraction. He couldn't pay attention... it seemed redundant and unnecessary.

As Elizabeth entered his room Tristan grabbed his blanket, the one that his Gram had made for him when he was a baby that *never* left his side, and doubled himself over. He held his stomach and whimpered. It was non-descript. It wasn't something a thermometer could measure. He could fake a stomachache... that would be easy. And, as anticipated, she came in, felt his forehead, and told him to rest and that he wouldn't be going to school today. Not in his condition. He fancied himself clever. He'd never gotten a chance to stay home unless he was actually sick. The day was all his for whatever he had hoped to make of it.

After a few hours, she was in her routine of cleaning and tending to his little sister. She was getting ready to turn two years old and wasn't much of a nuisance, but she also wasn't really his sister. Her father was not his father. His real father didn't live with them. Elizabeth left him for fear of her life. That's what she told the two of them, anyway. They lived in a small rancher just shy of 1,200 square feet. It had three bedrooms, the largest of which was all the way down the hall, on the opposite side of the house from the kitchen. The kitchen was where she and his little sister were. So, he crept out of bed, peaked through the crack of the door, and made a b-line down the hall into his mother's room. Their room was much more interesting than his.

It would be years later that he would understand what he was looking at that day, but for the sake of this story, it's important to disclose. On their nightstand sat a bong with marijuana residue, film vial cases filled with marijuana, and ashtrays staked with mountains of cigarette butts. This, of course, was not what he saw. In his little mind, they were all "off limits," as was so often communicated by his mother and stepfather. It was almost a verbal invitation for disobedient curiosity. How could they blame him for that?

Just next to the ashtray was a small, red Bic lighter. They were touted as childproof, but he had seen them lit on so many occasions that the challenge appeared possible. He grabbed the lighter and paced his way around their queen-sized waterbed. In the 1980s, waterbeds were apparently in style. He hated them. He couldn't jump on them, and therefore, they served no real purpose to him. So, he focused his efforts on the perimeter of the room and finally fixed his eyes on their closet door, slightly ajar with Christmas wrapping paper hanging out from within. That would be his target.

He thought for a minute about what might happen if his mother caught him out of bed. Would she yell at him for not being sick? Or would she be angrier that he was in her room? Of course, he was six. So, those thoughts fleeted as the temptation of the wrapping paper and the lighter in his hand grew.

It took him what seemed like an hour to get that lighter to spark into flame. It was, despite all previous confidence, nearly childproof. Nearly. When he did finally get a flame going, he moved it quickly to the edge of that wrapping paper that peered out of the closet in front of him, taunting him. At first the edge caught and stayed relatively contained. But that changed quickly as the fire ran into the dark of the closet where he could not see. Tristan panicked. And rather than opening the door to see what else might be in there, he quickly and quietly opened his parents' door, closed it softly, and ran down the hall back to his room... lighter still in hand.

Tristan opened his eyes, which at that point were glazed over with tears transcending twenty years of pain. He was still frozen in the same spot centered in that parking lot. He wondered how long he had been standing there. After surveying the cars around him, he realized no one had come or gone since the flashback had taken hold of his attention.

He took a deep breath. It had been so very long since the picture of that lighter had crossed his mind. Yet the memory moved so smoothly through his head, it was as if he was right there – with that little boy. He didn't remember him... the little boy, that is. His heart had since hardened over the years from all the trauma and mounting fear of his past. He glanced at his watch and realized he still had some time.

Tristan opened the car door to get a little fresh air. He was shaking. It felt uncontrollable. He closed his eyes to rest and collect himself, only to meet that memory right where he left it... sitting in his room with a red lighter still in his grasp.

He lay there in his bed while his little heart beat a mile a minute and, for the first time in a long time, felt truly scared of what might happen. He immediately hid the lighter under his mattress. There was no telling what might happen if he were to be caught with it still tightly grasped in his little hand.

"Please... please go out," he whispered to no one, rocking slightly on his bed. "I didn't mean it. I didn't mean it, I promise."

He pressed his tiny fists to his temples as if he could will the fire to disappear.

The seconds turned to minutes before the smoke alarm blared. He had only heard this once before, which is the only reason he even knew what it was to which he was listening. At the beginning of the year, they made the kids all do a fire drill. Before he could start to imagine what was happening down the hall, Elizabeth burst through the door, grabbed him (his stepsister in her other arm), and ran out of the house without so much as a coat. At this point, he was too scared to cry.

They stood across the street, too shocked to care about how insanely cold it was (though there was no snow on the ground), and watched their little home, all 1,200 square feet, burn down to nothing but ash. He couldn't take his eyes off the blaze. It was incredible. He'd never seen anything like it. They did eventually move indoors. Their neighbors ushered them in as firetrucks swarmed the street and blocked any entrance back to the house... what was left of it, anyway.

Days passed and his heart felt laden with a mix of fear and guilt. He obviously had no idea what was to become of their little home. He was so sorry. That's all he could think. And that was the extent of it... just thoughts. If his mother had found him out, there's no telling what kind of trouble he might be in. They had since moved into his grandparents' home (the parents of his stepfather), and for a short period of time life resumed as usual. He, of course, was elated to get back to school. Though predictable, it was safe and familiar and kept him far away from the day he set his home on fire. That, however, was all about to change.

A month had nearly passed since Tristan had burned down his home. He knew this only because it was close to Valentine's Day and he had his sights on the cards and candies they would get in class. It made the days tolerable. That morning, before school, his mother had sent his twin sister ahead to the bus stop with his grandmother. She was his stepfather's mom. Elizabeth wanted to talk to him. She knelt down with a serious but comforting face and asked him if he knew how the fire might have happened. A small part of him knew this was probably inevitable... there were only so many ways a fire like that could have ignited. He shook his head, however, and denied any part of it.

"Tristan," she said softly, kneeling to meet his eyes. "I need you to know... I believe you. But one day, if you remember something, you can tell me. I'll still love you. No matter what."

He nodded, but the lump in his throat burned worse than any flame. "I promise, Mom. I'll tell you."

Had it not been for the tears that began to stream down his face that may have been enough of a response. She knew better... and so did he. She refused to press him any further, and, after a gentle hug, she walked him to meet his sister at their bus stop.

School that day wasn't at all different than most, and his usual boredom ensued almost immediately after the first bell rang. He couldn't shake the feeling that the talk his mother had started just an hour ago wasn't over. He began to play through a few ways to explain away his actions. Nothing seemed legitimate enough for her. She could see right through him. It was one of the reasons their connection was so strong. There was no reason to keep ruminating over the conversation that would inevitably be picked up when he got home. It was best just to engage his schoolwork and forget about the whole thing... for now. He then started to think of Marie.

His sister wasn't in the same classroom. They were inseparable, and so the private school that their Gram insisted they attend thought it wise to broaden their social network and have them taught by different teachers. It was one of those schools that regarded themselves as progressive. They couldn't have been too smart, because each day both he and his sister found their way to one another. Perhaps it was a twin thing. Apparently, the things they say about the "twin connection" isn't altogether untrue. It wasn't until lunch, however, that she worked up the nerve to ask him what their mother wanted to talk to him about.

He wasn't sure how to respond to her. He had always been so honest with her; primarily because she was, at least on the surface, much more commonsensical and seemingly brighter. Needless to say, she wore the proverbial pants. His response was premeditated – and he knew her question would have something to do with the fire. He explained that their mom simply asked what had happened, and that she swore that whatever his response there would be no repercussions. She promised him more than once. With that response, for the second time that day, he lied to someone he loved.

The afternoon moved quickly. Lunch was followed by recess, gym, and then an afternoon of math. He was extraordinarily mediocre when it came to coordination. His sister, however, was not. She might as well have had the lion's share for the both of them. But, because their classes shared gym time, she made sure that he was on her team. It was the only way he wouldn't face the humiliation of being picked last. Again, most first graders are protected by such cruelty early in grade school. This was, as mentioned, a progressive school and they harped on the concept of making choices and having the convictions to stick to them. Despite her efforts, though, he was consistently the weak link. Maybe he might have been more interested in devoting time to honing his coordination had it not been for such an active mind. That thought seemed to make sense to him.

The final bell rang, and they both met at their usual spot, just near the flagpole in front of where all the buses congregated. Their bus was #51. He liked that number because when he inverted the digits it made the number 15, which is the product of 3 and 5. And, because his favorite number was 7, he associated 3 and 5 as the preceding numbers in a pattern that added two to the previous digit. So, 3+2 = 5. And 5+2 = 7. It made sense to him. That's how he saw the world. Everything had a numerical value: words, colors, even feelings. His world was an ever-shifting series of numbers. He assumed they might help him understand patterns in the way the world worked. And, moreover, how people worked.

This type of thinking only perpetuated Tristan's skewed perspective of himself. The stranger his thoughts, the quieter he got. He remembered his street address because it was 2 and he and his sister represented the same number. He memorized his phone number because the seven digits made an "L-shape." He counted everything, even words, in groups of 10. He felt so awkward even thinking about these things.

Marie broke the silence and began to yell for their mother, who was approaching the pole where they had been waiting for bus #51. His first thought was one of anger, in all honesty. *Who the heck gave her the location of their meeting spot* he thought to himself? This was covert information, and someone must have been spilling something. He would make a note to have a serious conversation with his sister once they were home. Sadly, they weren't going home. Well, at least he wasn't going home.

Elizabeth ushered the two of them to her blue station wagon but quickly recognized that their grandmother was in the other car. On any other ordinary day, this would be a welcomed surprise. She was so kind and, for two 6-year-old children, uninhibitedly generous. Marie didn't think much of it. For Tristan, her lack of skepticism was alarming. She was typically the one to pick up on strange situations that had no real prompting. It wasn't a holiday. It wasn't anyone's birthday. If that wasn't enough, their grandmother got out of the car and called for Marie. But, only Marie. Finally, a little bit of shock to throw twins into a full-on tailspin.

Marie looked at Tristan curiously and simply refused to go without him. He didn't need to say anything or refuse himself. She always made it easy for the two of them to remain together. Always. The voice of her grandmother, however, was stronger than usual with a curtness she hadn't experienced. Almost as if she was rushing to get out of there. Tristan, on the other hand, held his mother's hand with all the force he could muster.

"Mom, where's Marie going? Why can't we stay together?" His voice cracked as he gripped her hand.

"Just for today, sweetheart. Just for today."

"No! We're supposed to stay together. You promised!"

He screamed until his chest hurt, but the only thing that was left with her was his heart.

He watched as his grandmother, his stepfather's mother, gave him a half smile while escorting Marie into the backseat of her car. At the same time, Elizabeth assured Tristan that everything was going to be ok and to get in her car. He stared off at Marie wondering why they weren't riding together. Nothing seemed to add up.

His mother finally spoke up as she buckled herself in and explained to Tristan that they would be going back to the house while Marie and their grandmother would be doing a little shopping. It all made sense. If anxiety was a feeling Tristan understood, he would have told her then that her explanation eased his anxiety. His heart did, however, slow to a normal pace as he began to allow the circumstance to settle. *Perhaps Marie and their grandmother would grab him some candy* was the only thought that ran through his now excitedly creative mind. Nothing else seemed out of the ordinary.

The car ride wasn't very long. The house they used to live in before Tristan thought it fun to light wrapping paper on fire was a good distance from his school. Thankfully, his grandmother's house was much closer. He imagined to himself what snacks he'd dive into, how much homework he had, and what might be on the television. The fact that there was no conversation emanating from the front seat didn't at all occur to him.

As they pulled into his grandparents' development, he realized just then that Elizabeth had not said one word the entire ride. It was strange. They had a routine each day after school, which included questions about what he learned, what his favorite subject was (math, by the way... always math), and what his favorite teacher was like that day. None of those questions surfaced during their drive home. Aloof and content to run through the front door motivated by an afternoon snack, Tristan bolted from the car and headed toward the front door. His mother warned him before opening the door that there were two gentlemen waiting to meet him.

In that moment, everything clicked for Tristan. The irregularity of this afternoon's cadence suddenly surged to the forefront of his mind. And just like that, he lost his appetite.

Elizabeth opened the door and was greeted by two tall men in the foyer of his grandparent's home donning awkwardly fashioned sweaters. For some reason, Tristan paid attention to their sweaters. He wasn't particularly interested in clothes. But the cable knit, multi-colors in which these two men were cloaked imprinted on his eyes like a fourth of July sparkler. Perhaps it was because he'd never seen anyone wear a sweater like that. Or maybe it was simply because they were so darn ugly.

Breaking his eyesight away from their hideous apparel, Tristan looked up at his mother and noticed that she had started to cry. *Whatever is about to be said or done is not going to be good,* he thought to himself. And he was right.

Chapter 3

THE HOSPITAL

Tristan opened his eyes and once again looked at his watch. It was nearly time for his appointment. He was already exhausted after reliving the memory of the fire and the night he overdosed. His anxiety began to spike. Despite it all, he forced himself out of the car, across the parking lot, and through the front door of the church. The hallways were cloaked in biblical quotes, most of which he had remembered from his high school years when he began to learn about God. Yet, as he walked slowly and read each one, there was no heart response. Emotionally, he was walled off and felt at a loss as to why. It was just one of the many reasons why he found himself in that building.

He sat down in what he presumed was the waiting area and waited.

The thought of that day his mother broached the subject of the fire in the foyer of his grandparents' home left him blank and detached there in the lobby. For those passing by who gave him a quick glance, his stature boasted broad shoulders and a strong back, which accentuated his bad posture when he was seated. Anyone in this office would notice first his head hovering over his *lap with eyes clenched and an occasional tear drop. He couldn't shake the feeling that the encounter awaiting him on the other side of that door would require him to reveal himself entirely. Another tear fell.*

It wouldn't be hard to discuss and divulge only those things which brought him there. The lying, the distractions, and the incessant need for validation. That would be easy. He was remarkably impulsive and sought the next rush, whatever that may be. So, while his dreadfully misguided and thrill-seeking desire for impulse was the focus of this particular meeting, it was not the genesis. What precipitated his visit, which he would come to learn in the next hour, was so primal in nature that he couldn't bear the thought. His mind wandered to his wife and the idea of starting a family with her. How she managed to navigate these issues with him so patiently was beyond him.

A strong woman would have left by now. A lesser woman probably would have left a long time ago. She, of course, was neither of those. She understood how his mind worked better than he did. She would tell him that she saw who God had made her husband to be, and that was the thought that won out each time he would come home, tail tucked between his legs, ready to confess his latest mistake. Maybe that was why she stuck around. The heart and the head can sometimes misunderstand one another. His never seemed to be on the same page. Still, thinking of her and the hurt she was feeling, hurt he created, felt beyond impossible to manage.

With that, his mind began to wander back to that foyer twenty-seven years earlier. His tears were quickly replaced with anger.

February – 1988

There were some pleasantries exchanged between Elizabeth and the two older men standing there in his new temporary home. Not only were they unfamiliar, but they seemed quite cold. Tristan just sat there with both arms tied tightly around his mother's thigh with no intention of letting go. He figured he'd let them have their chat and move on with his afternoon. They were, after all, cutting into his premeditated snack and tv time.

Despite what seemed like, at least to Tristan, the end of the conversation, they moved over into the dining room and sat at the table. The two men took turns asking Tristan about his life. Their demeanors, while still a bit stoic, softened a bit. This encouraged Tristan to let his guard down and engage them as he would someone that his mother trusted. *Clearly, she trusts these guys* he thought to himself.

"Mom, why are we going so far?" he whispered, his eyes fixed on the unfamiliar skyline as the memory of that car ride returned.

"Just… somewhere that will help us, sweetheart."

"Help us do what?"

She hesitated. "Help you understand why the fire happened. And… to help me, too."

He turned to the window, pressing his forehead to the glass. "Will it hurt?"

She reached back and brushed his knee, voice soft. "No, baby. It won't hurt. I'll be right there."

It was less than ironic that his first response was to share everything about his twin sister. His interest was her. The "pretend play" in which they constantly engaged was typical for kids their age. The magical forests they had built in their minds were but a prelude to the adventures that always followed. In the most elaborate detail, he explained all of it. He went on and on about the dragon from *The Neverending Story* (a classic 80s movie you must see if you haven't already) and how each of them would scream for the dragon to come visit them in their backyard. It would be putting it mildly to say that their imaginations were robust and wildly creative. However, most of the imagination came from Tristan. It was his mind that would conjure these stories and scenarios that would take them on adventures lasting hours on end. While Marie carried most of the substance in their tandem, he did have the capacity to create these worlds for the two of them. Marie loved it.

As both men continued to listen, they grew increasingly aware of Tristan's language. A theme began to emerge, unbeknownst to Tristan. Both men took a brief second to talk among themselves before turning back to Tristan and addressing the interests he had spent the last five minutes sharing. They appeared extremely consumed with his use of the word "pretend" in his description of the way he and his twin played. Tristan was prepared to continue before being abruptly interrupted.

One of the men asked the boy, sitting there happily sharing his world with them, if he pretended a lot. His response was almost immediate. He absolutely pretended a lot. In fact, he spent most of his time thinking internally about the things he and his sister would get a chance to do later on. While he enjoyed toys and television and all the amenities the 1980s offered (including Nintendo), Tristan's mind was beautifully architected to create and develop and build and evolve. So, if an idea was introduced to him, it was inherent in his makeup to push that idea out further. To stretch it into something bigger and better and more enjoyable. He didn't know why he was this way. That didn't matter. What mattered was that it provided a love for magic and a means to challenge the impossible that both he and Marie enjoyed very much.

They then asked him something he didn't quite understand. An inquiry into a subject vastly beyond his depth of understanding. The question a*re you sad that your parents don't live together* seemed odd, even to a six-year-old. It was a leading question, but Tristan had no way of knowing that. It prompted a response that any child would evoke. *Of course, I'm sad* he pondered. *What a dumb question.* He thought more about why they would ask something like that. He suddenly found himself disinterested in the conversation. His smile faded, and almost immediately he got up out of his chair and went to sit on his mother's lap. As far as he was concerned, these men were no longer allowed to ask questions about his world.

It was almost as if the two of them were reading his mind, because as soon as Tristan sat down both men stood up and approached the door. *Good* he thought to himself. He felt they had worn out their welcome and he was ready to start the rest of his afternoon. But they would not be leaving... not without Tristan.

Elizabeth stood up and held her boy in her arms as she seemingly walked to let the two men out. Out of the corner of his eye, Tristan noticed a large suitcase sitting by the front door. He hadn't noticed it when he came home. It was likely because the ugly sweater men were blocking its view. Regardless, it caught him off guard. He looked at his mother with inquisition and a little fear. His initial thought was that she was going to go somewhere. Someplace with these men without him. It was quite possibly the worst thought that could have run through his mind. Unfortunately, the worst wasn't even on his radar.

She walked through the door and outside with the men holding more tightly than ever to Tristan. He felt safe when she squeezed him like that. It was as if nothing could get in the way. That is why what happened next didn't throw him off too much. She looked at him intensely and told him that they were going to be taking a drive with these men and that he could *rest assured* that everything was going to be alright. And with that, she sat Tristan in the backseat of the gentlemen's car and buckled his seat belt, only to buckle her own immediately after.

Rest assured. Those aren't words he would have understood when he was six, but the way his mother said it somehow provided context that made him feel comforted. He didn't know where they were going. She was careful with how she referred to their destination. But, in all of their back and forth, she convinced him that he was safe. She continued by explaining that their destination was full of really smart and imaginative people who were going to help him understand why he started that fire. He pleaded then, in the foyer, when he first admitted to it, that it was just curiosity. Why did it need to be more? Still, she insisted that there was something deeper and believed it would help him. He trusted her. He also trusted that when she said it was just for the weekend, that it was just for the weekend. In his mind, if she said it would only be a weekend and it would all be done, he would not argue. He told her everything in his short little life. All the things that might be considered worthy of secrecy. But, in that moment, he did not share with her that he was, in fact, afraid that he couldn't trust her this time.

She also told him that he wouldn't be alone. This comforted him. That car ride, which seemed longer than their family trip to Maine just a few months earlier, was bearable only because he knew she would be beside him the entire time. And with that, he sat quietly and observed the changing scenery as they approached Philadelphia. It wasn't anything he knew. The city was large and the streets were busy. He felt so small amidst the cars and the constant movements. The gentleman driving was the more talkative of the two just an hour or so earlier. During that car ride, however, he didn't say a word. Perhaps that's just as well. He didn't appear to be that friendly, anyway.

The city streets of Philadelphia felt like something of a mystery to young Tristan. There were grown-ups doing all kinds of weird things and acting in all kinds of weird ways. Yelling and falling down and acting silly. Tristan had no idea what he was seeing, but he didn't much fancy the view. He quickly turned to Elizabeth to hedge some of the ache beginning to well up in his belly. Anxiety. That's what Tristan was feeling. He was too young to be feeling such a strong emotion. Unfortunately, it would all too quickly become something of a common emotion that would impede his growth on several levels.

As they pulled up, the building seemed larger than life. He couldn't count the number of floors. He could only guess. And he tried. He enjoyed things like that; things that others couldn't, or perhaps wouldn't, think to think about. It was what made him different. Perhaps it's what prompted the fire. These thoughts suggested to him that maybe his mother was right. If he was curious about things like fire, and if this place could help him understand why he did what he did, there was a chance that it could help him understand why he did everything he did. In that moment he was no longer scared.

Elizabeth opened his door. She was tall and beautiful. Of course, most boys his age believe the standards of beauty and poise rise and set on their mothers, but he felt confident that this was especially true for her. Crawling out of the back seat he noticed her smile. It lacked a certain softness he'd grown used to. And just like that, he felt his stomach sink and that not so distant memory of fear settle back in. He wasn't an exceptionally perceptive boy... not in the way that others might understand. But he was sensitive. It was that sensitivity that persuaded his mind that something wasn't right about where he was. The building was slate gray, like a castle. And, unlike the other buildings surrounding this one, there weren't many people walking about. It was quiet and cold. Perhaps that's what he felt about his mother's smile. It, too, was quiet and cold.

But he held to the bond they shared. That was unbreakable by any standards. There was nothing that couldn't withstand the connection they shared. Not even a stone-cold building with floors too high to count. Nope, he would not focus on the things he couldn't control. He would only concentrate on the love and safety she pledged to him. So, he grabbed her hand and began to walk, clenching tighter to her with each progressive step.

The door at the entrance made a buzzing sound he'd never heard before. After that, a click as if something had been unlocked. The door then opened and behind it stood three men and one old, gray woman. She must have been as old as his grandmother. And she smiled like his grandmother. So, he immediately liked her. She was soft and was the first, and only, one of the four to speak. She prompted him to go with her and that his mother would be waiting in the other room.

"Mommy, no... no! You said you'd come with me... that you'd be right there!" His voice cracked as his fingered clutched her throat.

"I'll be right outside. I'm not leaving you."

"You're leaving. You're leaving me here with them!"

Tears ran down her face. "Only for a little while. You're so brave. I love you so much."

"Don't leave me, mommy. Please. I'm so sorry. I didn't mean it."

She let go of his hand and began to cry. He cried and screamed and yelled until the tears blurred his vision of her and she was gone. Perhaps she cried back an "I love you" from the outside of the door. But, if she had, he wouldn't have heard it. Not with all that screaming.

"Are you alright?" questioned a receptionist in the room where he was waiting. Tristan wasn't much for showing emotion and gathered himself quickly. Apparently, the last five minutes had taken him through memories that caused a constant stream of tears. That's what she, the woman at the patient check-in, told him, anyway. It felt real to him. As if he was right back there with that boy feeling what he was feeling all those years ago. He even went so far as to rub the sides of his face and neck to make sure there were no scars. It was one of the side effects of the fire. For months afterwards, nightmares

plagued him that he was left there to burn. That because the fire was his fault, he would have to deal with the consequences of his actions.

"How the hell did I get to this place," he thought. It wasn't as if he had chosen that institution. Had anyone clued him in on anything that was actually happening, he'd never allowed his mother to take him with those two men and their godawful sweaters. He learned over the years that his Gram, biological father, and aunt on his mother's side, made pushes to get him out of there, but to no avail. There was a larger motive beyond his three-month stint in the psychiatrist ward of the Children's Hospital of Philadelphia. He survived his first day, but just barely. And looking back, he was certain it wasn't going to get any worse. How could it? But this was not summer camp at the Y, and these people in here were absolutely insane.

The doctor is now 15 minutes behind schedule. He started to revisit that first night in the hospital. His eyes once again closed, and his mind began to race.

It had been nearly four hours since she had left him. He couldn't believe it. He was sure that she would come back for him at any moment. She promised. And she never broke a promise.

The first night was by far the worst for him. He was left with no concept of where he was or why he was there. Sure, there were orderlies and counselors probing the halls, but not one of them made him feel like he was supposed to be there. They barely communicated to him at all. He curled himself up in the corner of the common room where all of the "crazy kids" spent their free time and did nothing but observe them interact with one another. Tristan knew that his reference to them as "crazy kids" sounded harsh but was absolutely intentional. From where he was sitting, he was witnessing two kids yelling, face-down on the floor while two men held them down with their arms behind their backs. *How awful* was the only thing Tristan could think? Another boy who couldn't have been more than a couple of years older than he was busy throwing crayons and board games at another counselor. This was so far from normal to him. Perhaps "crazy" was the most appropriate word for everything he was seeing.

He was paralyzed by so many things, not the least of which was how lonely he felt. He'd never been by himself. Marie or Elizabeth or his grandmother were always no more than a modest yell away. But there he was, hours away from a family member or a friend, in a place he hated, left with nothing.

"Marie would know what to do," he whispered to the empty corner of the common room that first night. No one heard him. He pressed his face into his knees.

"She promised... she said just the weekend... she always promised..."

A shadow passed in the hall. He didn't look up. "I want to go home now. Please. Please take me home."

He wept on that chair, but only ever so quietly. He didn't want anyone to see him or sense just how scared he was. Not one child had come up to him to say even so much as a "hello."

He then heard what sounded much like the bells that sounded in his school, followed immediately by a woman's voice announcing that it was time for dinner. He just froze as everyone in the playroom exited out of the same door. He assumed they were going to get dinner, which was weird because he was always hungry. Not tonight, however. He wasn't hungry. He wasn't happy. He wasn't thirsty. He wasn't even sad. In that moment Tristan just became uncontrollably angry. He didn't deserve to be there. He had been tricked by his own mother. He hated everyone in that cold, cement-ridden hospital. And not learning to control and hide that anger would be the first of many mistakes he made that first night.

Tristan wasn't a defiant child. Far from it. If anyone was defiant, it was Marie. That girl would shout her disagreement with anything and to anyone. Sure, occasionally she might get a spanking, but the girl was made of nails. She felt no pain. Yet another reason why Tristan was happy to play second fiddle to her leading. She could handle being the first through the proverbial brick wall. He, on the other hand, buckled quickly at the first sign of adversity. He wanted peace and he wanted smiles. Life was that simple for him.

Understanding this about him is critical to understand why his first night in that hospital was so traumatic. He protested dinner, which didn't go over well but was still allowed. He supposed that he put up a good fight, but the reality was that he was still adjusting and the hospital staff knew that. They were happy to extend to him one free pass. Just one, unfortunately.

When it was time for bed Tristan, for the first time in front of anyone, began to sob without relent and with remarkable intensity. Everyone was staring. He didn't care. He screamed for Elizabeth and for Marie. He couldn't get a grip on himself. This went on for only a few minutes before one of the counselors felt it was time to introduce Tristan to the way they handled kids who got out of sorts in that hospital.

The next thing he knew, Tristan was on his stomach, hands locked, and arms shoved behind his back, with the full weight of a grown adult man on top of him.

Your temper tantrums won't help you here were the only words he could hear from the man leaning on him. He continued by letting Tristan know under no unclear terms that he'd better get used to being on his stomach.

That first night was the worst. Not because of the man. Certainly not because of the crazies with which he was surrounded. But because he felt alone. Truly and sufficiently alone. And, for the first time in his life, he lacked one thing he had always counted on: the predictability of safety.

Chapter 4

THE LIE

For months he was restricted to the confines of those stone-cold hospital walls, surrounded by some pretty disturbed children. That's all he could think about as the time continued to tick by sitting there, hunched over in the lobby of his yet-to-be seen counselor. Anger continued to stir within him. Where would he start? Tristan was troubled on so many levels. He lifted his head for a moment to wipe the tears and collect himself.

He noticed on the walls of the lobby in that church a picture of Jesus. At this stage of his life, these pictures evoked two very distinct feelings: hope and shame. He still didn't understand how God could fix this sorted mess, and so the shame would well up within him, overpowering the hope that gave him any fleeting sense of security.

A memory then surfaced. One so strong, painful, and explicit that he had nearly forgotten all about it. The mind is fascinating in that way. For Tristan, suppressing this specific event was the only way he was able to move forward after the hospital. Tears began to stream down his face as he remembered the gravity of the lie he was forced to tell. Everything changed after that. Everything.

April – 1988

The days felt like months, and the months felt like years. It was supposed to be a place of healing. From what, he still wasn't sure. He must have replayed the day of that fire in his little mind a thousand times working hard to pinpoint what went wrong and how he ended up in a mental institution. He had no way of knowing that a lighter and some wrapping paper would find him trapped in this inescapable prison.

His time there was remarkably routine. Twice a day he had group counseling with other kids his age. They would work their way around the room and each would share about the things they had done that had brought them to the hospital. The conversation always upset him terribly. Those around him would talk about their experiences causing harm to their pets or their little siblings. They would almost boast about the power and control they felt while doing so. It was painful to hear. And, for the most part, they didn't seem to have any remorse. They would reflect on their feelings of satisfaction when they saw others in pain. He didn't understand. It wasn't how he was wired.

Invariably, he would have to speak. They would all stare at him waiting for a story that emulated some of their own. The first few times Tristan refused to tell them anything but the truth. After all, he was not trying to hurt anyone. He wasn't angry. He wasn't crazy. He was simply enamored by the sight of the flames he created. He understood, even at a young age, the powerful nature of fire and how it intrigued him. What a misstep on his part. He wasn't concerned with fitting in, especially to the detriment of his truth.

"I'm not like you," he said once, so quiet it felt safer than thinking it.

And, especially with these people. They weren't like his friends at home. Of course, the others quickly picked up on his lack of interest in them or their stories. It was awful the way they would treat him.

When he initially arrived, Tristan was suffocated with the fear of the unknown. The environment was like nothing he had ever seen before, and the actions he witnessed were a far cry from anything he had experienced. These kids, however, gave him a slight sense of the familiar. They looked a lot like him and seemed to be interested in the same things Tristan enjoyed. In the common areas, there were board games and card games... plenty of things he was used to. Their ages ranged anywhere from Tristan's age to about 15 to the best that he could tell. But it would become glaringly apparent to Tristan that they were not like the friends he had at home.

These kids were hurting. They were products of abuse and pain. Some had burns from cigarettes put out on all visible parts of their little bodies. One girl, in particular, wore an eye patch. Her name was Katie. Katie was also in his twice daily counseling group. Tristan spent his first few days in the hospital with Katie, but because she was a girl, he had limited interaction with her. He did, however, get the opportunity to ask about her eye and that poor patch constantly covering it. That would be the first and last time Katie would ever talk to him. She told him that fighting with her older brother had never gotten serious before the day that he stabbed her with a butter knife. That was only after she took a pair of scissors to his stomach and drew first blood. Tristan was a lovingly compassionate boy. Sufficed to say, he had no response for Katie.

"I don't want to hear anymore," he murmured, staring at the scuffed floor until it blurred.

After that conversation, Tristan learned quickly not to ask anyone about what had happened to them. Not for any reason. Not ever.

But it was nothing compared to how those in charge would treat Tristan.

Each time he told the truth, the counselor would give him the opportunity to change his response. This never ceased to feel awkward and scary to Tristan. They didn't believe that he wasn't some type of pyro looking to burn down a home and destroy all semblance of normality in his little six-year old world. And, when Tristan would again tell the truth, he was *restrained*.

"Please, I'll be good," he cried into the carpet, his words lost in the sound of his own breath breaking.

Restraining kids in this hospital was an unfortunate commonplace. It wasn't different from what you might see in a prison; abuse of the most malicious sort. The counselors would work to force a response that accommodated their own understanding of what the truth should be. When that didn't happen, they would get angry. Tristan didn't do well with anger. He would lash out screaming all the reasons why he didn't belong in this godforsaken place. And, before he could blink, he was thrust onto his stomach and the counselor in charge would force his arms behind his back painfully and without relent. These restraints would sometimes last twenty minutes as kids would cry and struggle.

It wasn't something to which Tristan ever became accustomed. He was a gentle soul, and physical aggression wasn't part of his experience. At least, not until this hospital. Each time he would find himself stomach down on that floor it felt as though his arms might break. The physical pain, however, ran a distant second to the emotional fear that continued to grow inside him. He didn't understand it then, but a hardening began around his once beautifully pure and unfiltered heart.

The concept of this kind of physical reprimand redefined cruelty. It was also extremely eye-opening. Tristan knew he had no power. Truth was not going to set him free. In fact, it was the one thing keeping him locked away.

In this place love was weakness and kindness led to horrific abuse.

Tristan couldn't stop crying. That faucet was now fully engaged as his mind raced to the unfortunate clarity surrounding the late nights in that hospital bedroom. He tried to lift his head and break away from the memory in which he found himself trapped. It was flowing out of him uncontrollably. His eyes remained closed as one of those nights began to burn in his mind's eye.

Tristan never struggled to sleep. He loved to dream and felt at peace. Until now. While there were four kids to each room, partitioned by nothing more than two small dressers splitting the room in half, Tristan's bed was positioned in a manner where he could see the boy just across the room. His name was Hector. He'll never forget that name. Hector was 13 years old. He was the oldest boy in the room, and clearly the worst, at least toward Tristan.

While the abuse started during that first week in the hospital, the progression of its dysfunction accelerated quickly during that last month. Initially, he would sit in his bed and make Tristan watch. Hector never left his own bed but incessantly whispered to Tristan to continue looking his way. Tristan tried to keep his eyes closed but was always scared of what Hector might do if he didn't. It was too much for a child to see. Despite his age, Tristan knew that in those moments he was losing a part of himself. He could feel the change. It was alarming how aware he was.

The last night it ever happened was the most damaging. Tristan managed to nod off to sleep only to wake up to Hector at the foot of his bed. Hector had never left his own bed before. Tristan was frozen with fear. He could only sit and endure as Hector continued. That night Tristan's innocence was stolen.

Some may have considered what transpired next as an act of God, intervention for all those months of perverse exposure. But one of the other boys on the other side of one of those dressers caught a glimpse of the fear on Tristan's face and saw, firsthand, what Hector was doing. That next morning Hector was removed from the room, never to be seen again.

"He's still here," he whispered to himself that night, even though the bed was empty.

Despite the temporary reprieve, Tristan was aware that the damage had been done. The staff must have called and apprised his parents of the situation, because the next thing he knew they were both there waiting for him as Tristan was escorted to the visitation hall. He saw his mother, felt his heart drop, and began to weep. Emotions he didn't understand in a place that just continued to grow in dysfunction swept over him like a hurricane. He begged her to take him home. He promised never to touch a lighter again. He pleaded with both his biological father and his stepdad. He saw the tears in their eyes. And, in that moment, he knew his efforts were empty. His was the property of this hospital until they deemed otherwise. For all intents and purposes, his parents were just as paralyzed as Tristan.

Thankfully, the interactions with Hector would quickly prompt the hospital staff to offer an alternate living situation for the remainder of his stay.

Towards the end of the third month the hospital permitted his mother to join Tristan in an apartment set aside specifically for parents with children in the psychiatric wing. His heart was full once more. Despite her having left him there with strangers and no sense of safety, he longed for the love and security she provided. She was his world. And she could save him. For that, he could forgive her anything. He just wanted the nightmare to end.

As the days continued and the monotony of the routine grew tired, Tristan found himself sobbing to his mother, beseeching her to get him out. Unfortunately, it was now out of her control. She couldn't do anything about it.

"But you're my mom," he said, as if that fact alone could break the locks on the doors.

According to the professionals, he was a threat to himself and to others and would need a rational and rectifiable excuse related to the fire he started. *What excuse do I have but the truth* he thought to himself? He just didn't understand the world in which he lived. To the hospital psychiatrists and counselors, Tristan must have had a troubled past or behavioral issue to have incited such an awful act as serious as a fire. He, from their perspective, must be just like every other child in that hospital.

This insanity would have likely continued had it not been for his mother. She was brilliant. Not the type of brilliance people threw around when speaking of people or ideas that appeared novel only to them. Rather, she was actually brilliant. A tested, tried and true genius. She wrote music. She wrote literature. She seemingly had no limits. And, to his twin sister and him, the sun rose and set on her ability to make the world feel small and attainable. She drew people close to her with a gravity they couldn't understand.

Maybe that's why there was no reason for him to overthink it when she presented him with a thought that inspired a new, real hope for Tristan.

One idea, a simple mistruth, and the chance to escape the hospital suddenly became possible. To this day Elizabeth would tell you that she did it for her son. She would explain that she prompted the idea as a way of getting to some possibilities that could explain his incentive to set that fire. Perhaps her motivation was good. The fallout from the idea, however, would echo for decades and unleash an instability in Tristan that neither of them could have anticipated.

And so, the plotting began. Of course, the concept of *plotting* felt unfamiliar to Tristan. It wasn't like they were building a fort in the backyard or teaching him to play checkers. What they were doing was much more profound, even if they weren't really aware of its long-term significance. He honestly had no idea what might come out of her mouth. She approached the subject of the fire with Tristan in a very simple manner. It was the first time in a while that the two of them had discussed it. There was, after all, so much that had transpired in those short three months that would, in and of itself, have been enough for intensive therapy.

She then asked him a question. It seemed benign enough at the time. It pertained to his biological father and the time Tristan and his sister spent with him every other weekend. At first, Tristan didn't think much of it. They had never, not once, discussed his time with Peter, his father. When they did talk about him, it would typically be him or his twin who would regale their mother of the 7-Eleven Slurpee runs and venison stew dinners. They adored Peter. He was a wonderfully caring man. He loved his children. And, he had plenty to love. Apart from the twins, Peter fathered two other children and was a stepparent to three additional. Some could argue that he was perhaps a bit transient in his relationships. But that would have nothing to do with the kind of father he was. And, to all of his children, biological and step, he was the strongest and most loving man alive.

The question, after giving it some thought, began to cloud Tristan's sense of center. He didn't quite understand manipulation or the concept of being "led" in a conversation, but the question evoked a need to respond in a way he had never once considered. He immediately felt uneasy. At that young age, his heart was placed in a position somewhere between fear and guilt. It's not something any child should have to experience. He was, however, desperate. Desperate to leave the place that sufficiently corrupted his sense of virtue. If this was a way out, he was willing to do what was asked.

He couldn't know then that the words he was encouraged to speak with confidence and false honesty would change the course of his life forever. What he was led to help create would not only hurt him but would negatively reverberate in his life for decades.

Tristan opened his eyes to the sound of a door opening as he drew his mind away from that horrible day when the lie was born. His heart was heavy and beating quickly. There was sweat everywhere. From an on-lookers perspective, he might have been in the midst of a panic attack. Or perhaps he was just beginning to feel latent emotion from years of pain pushed way deep down. Regardless, he welcomed the distraction.

He had hoped it was his time to walk inside that door and begin vocalizing all of these memories. It was beginning to weigh too heavily on his heart. The shame of it all. The pain of it all. It was more than he was willing to take on. His poor wife. That's all he could think about. She was on the receiving end of so much garbage and he knew it. He loved her so much. His past, however, had obscured his ability to communicate that sufficiently and honestly.

As he looked up, he noticed the outline of what he assumed to be his counselor. But, as quickly as it had opened, the door was shut. He was, again, left in that waiting room with only his thoughts to keep him company. He had hoped for a reprieve from reliving that moment all those years ago. Alas, there was no such luck. And just like that, his mind fell back into the boy and his lie.

As he lay there in the comfort of his mother's arms, she began to unveil her thoughts. Elizabeth loved her Tristan dearly. It would not be a stretch to say that at that stage of her life, however, even she didn't understand the gravity of the questions she would plant in his impressionably helpless mind. What's more is what would transpire in the days and weeks to follow. It was unchartered territory for the both of them.

The start of the conversation centered more on a rehashing of the fire and how his eventual move to the hospital had nothing to do with her. To this day, Tristan doesn't know the truth. He couldn't know her motivation... not really. What was clear, however, were the words *this will get us all out of here.* She must have said them a hundred times during that embrace if she said them once. She had his full attention.

It's important to express the level of connection Tristan shared with Elizabeth. You may, as a mother or a father, appreciate the indelible bond created between children and their parents at a very early age. For Tristan, you could take the strength of that bond, stretch it to the depths of forever, and still barely have an understanding of just how inseparable they were. There are so many ways to elaborate on the enormity of their relationship, so many analogies that could be drawn.

Imagine your child or your mother or father. Imagine your heart beating in like rhythm with theirs. Imagine every fundamental need hanging on the moves they made. Tristan and Elizabeth were this way. Beautifully connected. Sharing one heart. He was her boy. She was his lifeline. So, you can imagine, then, how remarkably difficult it was for him to be away from her for as long as he had until the day she arrived in that apartment. Regardless of the consequence, she could never steer him in a wrong direction.

Do you feel safe on the weekends when you're with your daddy was a startling question for Tristan to hear. He wasn't sure how to respond to something so flagrantly simple. *Of course I feel safe,* he thought to himself. What a strange question. What a strange question coming from her. She knew full well how he felt about his father. He would tout about the buck his father shot over the weekend and mull on and on about how he learned to properly skin and clean a deer. How to respect the animal. Why it was important to respect the animal. His father spoke to him as if he was an equal. It always made Tristan feel so special. So unique.

That was one of the most endearing traits about Peter... at least to Tristan. He was the only boy in a house full of sisters. Stepsisters. Half-sisters. And, of course, his twin sister. There was a type of bond he shared with his father that no one else had the opportunity to experience. Not only did he feel safe with his father, but Tristan felt understood. And there was a small part of him that knew, despite his age, that a boy's bond with his father is beyond unbreakable. Tristan secretly coveted this. And, even if it was only in his mind, he felt Peter coveted it, too. Which, as you will come to learn, was how the lie would physically and emotionally change both of their hearts forever.

He sat there for a moment and began to think about his father. Peter had come to visit his son in the hospital every week, without fail, for the last three months. Tristan loved him dearly. And, while he wasn't able to see him every day as he did his mother, he understood that the circumstance had nothing to do with him. At an age that young, it was exceptional that he could grasp the concept of two sets of parents. So, the thought continued to surface inside his mind; *why is mom asking me this?*

He finally spoke up to Elizabeth after what felt like an hour of inner monologue and quickly communicated that he did feel safe. Very safe. He went on to tell her, without prompting, that his daddy was a wonderful daddy. That Tristan was truly lucky. That his sister was lucky. As he continued, Elizabeth just sat quietly and listened. With each word flowing out of his mouth, her face relaxed a bit, and he began to feel at ease again. But then she spoke again. And, this time, just three little words.

Are you sure?

At six years old, very few children would be able to process the implications and subtext stemming from those three short words. Somehow, however, Tristan did. He could see it in her eyes. He could feel it in her arms. She didn't say anything more than that. Not one more word. And, she didn't have to. Clearly this was her way of creating his out.

"What if I just tell them what you want?" he asked, not knowing which answer would make her smile.

Suddenly, Tristan found himself immersed in the fear of the unfamiliar. Of course, Peter was as significant as any father was to any boy. But Elizabeth was his entire world. If Peter represented the strong arm of Tristan's young body, then his mother would undoubtedly be his heart. Tristan knew he could manage a life without an arm. His heart, however, he could never live without.

He glanced at his mother with a curious look. She interrupted his soon-to-be racing mind with comments and scenarios that would later represent the web of lies they would both begin to spin. He had no idea what was happening.

That moment turned from minutes to hours, during which time Tristan became something he never thought he would ever become... a liar. That night, for the second time in his life, and all inside 90 short days, Tristan burned down another home. Unfortunately, this home would not be rebuilt. It could not be salvaged. It would not be covered by insurance or be met with friendly faces with arms outstretched holding meals and toys. The house he burned down was his family's heart.

Everyone would feel pain because of it. Everyone he knew would be affected by his lie. And, for the ensuring few years, the emotional anguish he internalized would manifest itself in ways no one could predict.

Just. One. Lighter. That's all it took.

Chapter 5

CHILDHOOD, TAKE 2

is eyes burst open. He sat for just a moment and then stood up, faced the door, and exited that church building without so much as the slightest of hesitations. He had been waiting for too long. He had spent too much time in his own mind. And for what?

He was so tired. Reliving the memories that had plagued him for so many years felt like a sprint and a marathon all at once. It was so hard. He walked through the door and felt the frigid air brush his face, drying the perspiration that coated each pore. He could see his car, alone in the parking lot, and was reminded of his own loneliness. In that instant, his purpose for being there rushed back with vigor. It was, of course, because of her. And with that, he stopped. Turned around. And walked back into the church.

It was not of his own volition. Any strength he might claim to be his own had long since left him. This was something else, or someone else, that was prompting him to face it all. Before he knew it, he was back in that chair and immersed in a new string of memories. Thankfully, it was quieter. His mind's eye had taken him past the time in the hospital. And thank God for that.

The Move – Fall, 1988

The move was swift and deliberately final. One minute, he was navigating the familiar streets of a neighborhood that held the ghost of Peter's footsteps, and the next, he was standing in the middle of a box-filled living room in a new state, the air heavy with fresh paint and forced beginnings. It was a clean break—too clean. The house was beige and uninspired, nestled at the end of a cul-de-sac with trimmed hedges and neighbors who waved but never really looked.

They told him it was for the best. That they needed space. That sometimes families had to make hard choices. But Tristan knew.

"If it's for the best," he asked one night over dinner, "how come nobody looks happy about it?"

His mother didn't answer right away. She took a slow sip of her coffee instead, her eyes fixed somewhere past the window.

"Some things don't feel good until later," she finally said.

"Later" sounded a lot like "never."

Even at eight, he understood that this wasn't about opportunity. It was about disappearance. It was about putting enough distance between their new lives and the man who might still believe he was part of theirs.

He started third grade without ceremony. A new school, a new district, a new chance to rewrite himself. His teacher—her name never stuck—was kind in the way adults are when they know too much but pretend otherwise. She gave him space. Let him linger at the edge of activities. Greeted him each morning with a smile that held just enough softness to feel sincere.

No one asked about the hospital.

No one whispered when he walked past.

And for a while, that was everything.

He faded into the background by choice. Avoided raised hands, shrugged through group projects, found solace in the predictability of worksheets and silent reading. He learned the patterns quickly—who to sit near, who not to. How to nod just enough during lessons so he wouldn't be called on.

There was comfort in the ordinary. After the chaos, the institutions, and the unrelenting scrutiny of professionals and parents alike, being overlooked felt like safety.

And for the first time in as long as he could remember, Tristan allowed himself to exhale.

The Gift

Fourth grade arrived with little fanfare. The supplies were familiar: composition notebooks, capped glue sticks, pencils sharpened to their nerves. But Tristan entered differently. Taller, slightly more withdrawn, quiet in a way that no longer stemmed from fear alone. He had learned to disappear in plain sight. But something had changed, something had awakened inside him—and it began to show.

The first signs were subtle. He remembered entire passages from his reading textbook, reciting them word for word days after closing the cover. He spotted numerical patterns others couldn't see and solved math problems in seconds. At first, he thought it was normal. It didn't feel special. It just *was*—like his eyes had grown sharper or his ears more attuned. But his teachers noticed. Quickly.

They pulled him aside. Called his mother. Used words like "gifted," "advanced placement," "off the charts." Tristan didn't know what any of it meant, only that it made people look at him differently. The kind of different he had spent the last year avoiding.

His mother, true to form, latched onto the news like a drowning woman grabbing rope. She had always claimed there was something exceptional about him, something unusual— now she had proof. She began talking louder, smiling wider, retelling the story of his brilliance to anyone who would listen. He watched her drink in the attention, as if *his* gift confirmed *her* worth.

But at school, things got harder. His teacher, well-meaning but overwhelmed, started isolating him from the others. "You finish so fast," she would say, placing yet another advanced packet on his desk. "Try this while the others catch up." It sounded like praise. It felt like exile.

"Can't I just wait for everyone else?" he asked once, pushing the packet back toward her.

"You'd be bored," she said without looking up from the stack of papers in her hands.

"Maybe bored is better," he murmured, more to himself than to her.

She smiled like she hadn't heard the question, which was somehow worse than no.

And the lie—the big one, the one he had carried since the hospital—pressed heavier on his chest. Peter's absence was no longer an event but an erasure. His name never came up. The house was void of any evidence he'd existed. And yet, the memory of him burned so vividly inside Tristan's mind that it felt almost cruel. To remember so perfectly something you were told to forget. That was the curse of this gift.

His memory sharpened by the week. Every classroom moment, every accidental comment, every tension between his mother and stepfather etched into his brain like carvings in wet cement. He couldn't forget even if he wanted to.

"Does everybody remember stuff like this" he asked a boy from his class during recess, naming off the colors of every shirt they'd seen that day.

The boy laughed like it was a game. "I don't even remember what I had for breakfast."

"Pancakes," Tristan said automatically. "With syrup on your sleeve."

The boy stopped laughing.

But even with the gift, something was missing. There were questions no one answered. Restlessness that no packet could cure. By October, he had started faking mistakes. Taking longer on tests. Pretending not to know what he already did. He thought maybe if he seemed more normal, he could be left alone again.

It didn't work.

Instead, he was pulled into meetings. SAT words whispered over his head. "Cognitive thresholds," "accelerated learning tracks," "possible testing for placement." He began to wonder if he'd ever feel ordinary again—or if that chance had been permanently stripped from him.

And then, in a small conference room with gray carpet and bad lighting, they introduced him to someone new. A man not affiliated with the school, but with the local university. Someone who asked to speak with him directly.

"Do you like puzzles?" the man asked, his smile both serious and kind.

Tristan nodded.

And with that, something opened.

The Professor

His name was Everett. He never asked Tristan to call him "Mr." or "Professor" or anything formal. Just Everett. He didn't dress like the other adults at school. He wore threadbare sport coats with elbow patches and carried a satchel that looked like it had been dragged through a decade of chalk dust and philosophy lectures. His shoes were always untied. His thoughts never were.

They met twice a week in the library, in a small alcove carved out near the back with two chairs and a chalkboard no one used anymore. Everett never brought worksheets. He never started with "let's review." Instead, he slid chessboards between them, dropped math riddles onto scraps of paper, and once opened a session with a diagram of the Fibonacci spiral drawn on the back of a napkin.

"What do you see?" he asked that first day, sliding a complex numerical sequence across the table.

"Patterns," Tristan said slowly. "But they're not finished. Like they're waiting for me to do something to them."

Everett leaned back. "What would happen if you didn't?"

Tristan frowned. "Then they'd just sit there. Like... lonely numbers."

"Lonely numbers," Everett repeated, almost to himself. "That's not in the math textbooks."

Tristan stared. Not at the numbers, but at the question itself. What do you *see*?

It changed something in him. Not what he knew, but how he approached knowing.

Everett didn't rush. He asked questions that had no single answer. He let silence sit for minutes without flinching. He introduced words like *epistemology* and *intuitionism*, and expected Tristan not to memorize them, but to wrestle with them.

And Tristan did.

He felt his mind stretch in those sessions. Not like a balloon inflated too far, but like a landscape widening just beyond the horizon. Everett didn't treat him like a prodigy. He treated him like a peer. Someone to be explored, not explained. And Tristan, for the first time, stopped shrinking.

They talked about paradoxes, algorithms, and the theory of infinity. But they also talked about books, the color of thought, the morality of knowledge. Once, Everett handed him a worn copy of *Flatland* and said, "You'll understand this before most grad students do."

But it wasn't just about the content. It was about the context.

Everett asked about *how* Tristan learned, not just what he learned. He noticed patterns in his thinking. He traced connections others missed. He once called his mind "an unmarked map with deep rivers running underneath."

And when the sessions ended, Everett never offered compliments. Only invitations.

"Next time, bring your questions."

"I already have some," Tristan said, leaning forward. "But I don't think they're about math."

Everette Smiled faintly. "The best ones usually aren't."

"What if I ask something and there's no answer?"

"Then you'll have to learn to live in the space between the question and the answer," Everett said. "Most people spend their whole lives avoiding that space. You might as well get comfortable."

That was the kind of praise Tristan lived for.

By the spring, the librarian had started leaving snacks out for them. The custodian stopped vacuuming near their table during sessions. It was like a small part of the world had folded open just for them.

And in that quiet, deliberate space, Tristan began to feel like himself—not the broken boy with too many diagnoses, or the genius child with too much pressure.

Just himself.

Seen. Stretched. Understood.

Miss Scarlett

Fifth grade came with a strange sense of peace. Not joy, not ease—but a peace shaped by the contrast of everything that had come before. The nightmares had dulled into faded echoes. The black-and-white panic of hospital corridors had softened into color. And for the first time, Tristan entered a new classroom not afraid, but curious. Curious if it might actually last.

Miss Scarlett was waiting at the door.

She wasn't dramatic or overly warm. She didn't clap her hands or belt out morning greetings. Instead, she offered a nod. A look. One that said, *I see you.* Not just your name on a roster, not just your test scores from last year. *You.*

There was something grounded about her. She wore thick glasses and long cardigans with fraying cuffs. Her hands were always ink stained. Her desk looked like a used bookstore had exploded on top of it. And she never once raised her voice. She didn't have to. Her presence alone was enough.

Tristan found his seat near the window, and by lunchtime, he had met Conor.

He had the kind of smile that arrived before his words. Messy hair, an overactive pencil tapping habit, and a running commentary about everything the teacher said. "Scarlett's a secret genius," he whispered to Tristan during math. "She has like, a thousand books in her house. I bet she's a wizard."

"If she is," Trusted muttered back, "I hope she knows a spell for making people leave you alone."

"Why would you want that," Conor asked, edging closer.

Tristan hesitated. "Because sometimes it's easier not to be found."

Conor grinned like that was the best answer in the world, but he didn't push.

Tristan didn't laugh right away. But Conor didn't seem to mind. He kept talking, kept sitting next to him, kept offering half his Pop-Tart during recess without ceremony.

By the end of the week, Tristan had laughed. Twice.

Miss Scarlett noticed. Of course she did.

She paired them for reading projects. Let them work together during science labs. And when Tristan finished assignments early, she didn't hand him more worksheets—she gave him journals. Told him to write. Anything. Everything. No rules.

It was the first time he had ever been invited to let his mind wander freely.

And somehow, she still kept her distance. She didn't pry. Didn't probe his story. But every once in a while, she said things like, "You know, you don't have to be perfect to be brilliant," or "Some people survive by hiding. That doesn't mean they're small."

He never responded. But he heard her.

With Conor beside him and Miss Scarlett behind him, the classroom became something it had never been before: safe. And not just because it was quiet, or consistent. But because, for once, it felt like the people in it weren't trying to fix him or figure him out. They were just letting him be.

And for a while, that was enough.

He didn't know it yet, but the ground was already shifting again. The blackouts would come. The silence would return. But that fall—those first months of fifth grade—they were his.

And even now, years later, he could still remember the exact way the sunlight hit Miss Scarlett's chalkboard when she introduced haikus. He could still remember the sound of Conor's pencil tapping as he tried to find a rhyme for "fortitude."

It was the closest thing he had to normal.

And that made it sacred.

The Blackouts

It started on a Tuesday.

Tristan had been staring at a clock on the classroom wall, watching the second hand tick and tick and tick. The next thing he knew, he was in the hallway, standing in front of a row of lockers with no memory of how he'd gotten there. The bell hadn't rung. No one had called his name. He just... wasn't where he used to be.

At first, he thought it was stress. Or maybe he had just zoned out. But it happened again two days later. This time during science, while labeling the parts of a flower. He looked down and realized his worksheet was finished—correctly—but he had no memory of filling it in.

Then came the gaps. Minutes. Then entire class periods. Missing time like holes punched into the day. Teachers began to notice. So did Conor.

"You okay, dude?" he asked during lunch. "You looked like you saw a ghost in art."

Tristan nodded quickly. Too quickly.

He didn't want to talk about it. He didn't want to give it power. But it kept happening.

Miss Scarlett noticed, of course. She saw him lose focus—not just the wandering kind, but the gone kind. Eyes glazed. Face blank. Present in body but absent in every other way. She began to adjust things gently. Moved his seat. Asked him grounding questions at transitions. Never in front of the others. Always with care.

"Where did your thoughts go just now?" she'd whisper as she handed him a book.

"Somewhere I don't want to go," he said quietly, "but I can't remember leaving here to get there."

"What's it like there?" she asked, her voice low enough that no one else could hear.

"Like the part in a story where the page is missing, but you're still supposed to know what happened."

She didn't write anything down. She just nodded.

He didn't know how to answer. Because he didn't know where he went.

The school counselor chalked it up to anxiety. Said it might be a response to trauma. They used words like *dissociation, emotional overwhelm, repressed memory*. All Tristan knew was that it felt like parts of his life were being borrowed without permission. And no one told him when they'd be returned.

The episodes grew more frequent in December. One moment he'd be writing a poem. The next, standing by the window with a pencil snapped in half. Miss Scarlett never panicked. She adjusted. Adapted. Held the boundaries tight but gentle.

Then came the incident in math class.

He was mid-sentence, explaining a pattern, when his voice trailed off and his hand dropped. He sat completely still for three full minutes, breathing, blinking—but unresponsive. When he returned, the room had shifted. Everyone was quiet. Miss Scarlett was crouched beside him, one hand on his desk, her eyes full of something that looked like deep understanding. Or maybe sorrow.

She called home that night.

His mother reacted exactly as she had before.

The following day, Tristan found his overnight bag already packed. The same one they had used the last time. There was no conversation. No explanation. Only her voice, bright and hollow: "Just for observation, baby. We'll get some answers. It'll be good for you."

It was her pattern. When things got too complicated, she didn't ask for help—she outsourced the responsibility.

And once again, Tristan became the problem to be solved.

The Second Stay

The new facility was tucked behind a row of aging medical buildings, as though someone had tried to hide it in plain sight. It lacked the severe gray edges of the last institution. This one was quieter. Smaller. With beige carpeting that muffled every footstep and pastel-colored bulletin boards that tried too hard to be cheerful. It smelled like lemon cleaner and suppressed feelings.

His mother had said it would just be a few weeks. That they only needed to "figure a few things out." That this was the best way to get ahead of whatever was happening. But she hadn't looked him in the eye when she said it. She had folded and refolded the same scarf three times as she spoke, her words practiced, her voice glossy and forced.

Tristan didn't argue.

He had learned long ago that resistance only prolonged the inevitable. And besides, something in him—some tired, frayed strand—was almost grateful for the silence that came once the door clicked shut behind her. At least here, no one expected him to pretend everything was fine.

He had done this before.

He knew the intake routine. The shallow questions. The dull clipboard scratches. The impersonal once-overs by clinicians who called him "buddy" or "kiddo" in a tone that always made him feel smaller than he was. He knew the rooms—single beds with navy wool blankets that never quite kept out the cold, plastic dressers too light to cause harm, windows that didn't open.

He learned the schedule quickly. Morning vitals. Group therapy. Individual sessions. Recreational hour with poorly inflated basketballs and puzzle pieces that never fully fit. The other kids didn't speak much at first. Some rocked gently in their chairs. Others stared past him, as if their eyes had moved permanently inward. He recognized that look.

He kept to himself, but he watched.

He watched everything—the way the nurse on night shift always smoothed out the corners of his chart even when no one was looking. The way the boy in the room across the hall hummed the same four-note melody before every meal. The way no one ever sat in the orange chair near the TV, even though it was the most comfortable one.

He watched, and catalogued, and waited.

And then, on the second Tuesday, Miss Scarlett arrived.

She walked through the locked double doors like she belonged there. No hesitation. No awkward smiles. She had a messenger bag over one shoulder and a paperback novel tucked beneath her arm. Her scarf was crooked, her boots wet from the rain, and her face entirely calm.

She looked at him like nothing had changed.

"Tristan," she said, nodding slightly. "We've got some work to do."

He blinked. For a moment, he wasn't sure if he was imagining her. But she set her bag down at the visitation table and started pulling out worksheets, vocabulary cards, and a stack of graded assignments with his name written in her precise, looping cursive.

"I told the school I'd handle your classwork personally," she said, sliding a pencil toward him. "We've still got that short story unit to finish. And Conor said you'd be mad if you missed his final poem."

Tristan sat down, slowly. Carefully. Like one wrong movement would break the spell.

But it wasn't a spell. She really was there.

She came every Tuesday and Thursday, without fail. Rain or sun. Late or early. She brought lessons and questions and an absurd number of highlighters. But more than that, she brought the outside world in. She was a bridge—between the version of him trapped inside those padded walls, and the version of him who still believed he could become something more.

And she never treated him like a patient.

She never once asked why he was there. Never pried. Never hinted at pity. Instead, she talked about books. Asked about characters. Debated the rhythm of poetry and the ethics of protagonists. She gave him a clipboard once with a story prompt— "Write about a door that doesn't lock"—and said nothing else.

He filled six pages.

The nurses started calling her "the English lady," though they whispered it with a kind of reverence, like she was an apparition who might not stay. But she stayed. Week after week. And somehow, her presence shifted everything.

Even the other kids noticed. A few of them lingered outside the visitation room when she arrived. One day, the boy who hummed in four-note loops handed her a crumpled drawing and said, "You look like someone in a story."

Tristan didn't say it, but he had thought the same thing.

Her presence reminded him that the world outside hadn't forgotten him. That school still existed. That someone had noticed his absence—and cared enough to show up.

And it wasn't just her. He received a folded note one afternoon during a session with the counselor. It had been left with the front desk. The handwriting was jagged, almost unreadable.

"You better come back soon. I'm sick of beating everyone at four square. – Conor."

Tristan read it twice. Then three times.

It was the first time in weeks that he smiled.

He didn't know how long he'd be there. No one told him. The blackouts hadn't returned. His therapist spoke in circles— phrases like "emotional recalibration" and "self-regulation strategies"—but he didn't mind. He wasn't waiting on them to fix him.

He was holding on to something else now.

Tuesday and Thursday afternoons.

The sound of Miss Scarlett's boots on linoleum.

A scribbled note from a best friend.

A clipboard with stories that didn't need to be true to feel real.

Gratitude

They released him in late April. No grand ceremony. No final meeting filled with definitive answers. Just a printed discharge form, a half-hearted smile from the lead therapist, and a brown paper bag containing his sketchbook, two paperback novels, and the pencil Miss Scarlett had insisted he keep.

The ride home was silent. His mother didn't ask questions, and he didn't offer answers. She had perfected the routine of extraction—of pulling him from one world and inserting him into another without so much as a ripple. But this time, Tristan didn't resist the silence. He simply watched the scenery pass by, mile after mile, cataloging the trees, the road signs, the shadows, as though he could anchor himself to the world again through observation alone.

When he walked into school that Monday morning, everything looked the same—but he wasn't. There was something heavier in his walk, something sharper behind his eyes. But as he turned the corner toward his classroom, Conor appeared.

"Dude."

That was all he said. But the grin that followed was pure sunlight.

Before Tristan could say a word, Conor had wrapped his arms around him in the most uncoordinated, impulsive, lopsided hug imaginable. It was the kind of hug that said *you disappeared and it scared me and I don't know how to say that, so I'm just going to hold you until it makes sense.*

"I saved your seat," he said, pulling back. "And your spelling list is a joke this week. You'll be fine."

Tristan blinked once. Then smiled.

He hadn't realized how deeply he'd missed being missed.

The rest of the day passed in fragments. Miss Scarlett greeted him without comment, only a soft hand on his shoulder and a subtle shift in her voice when she read aloud to the class. Conor passed him a note during writing period: *We've got catching up to do. Like, serious Pop-Tart level catching up.*

72

Tristan wrote back: *Do they still make brown sugar cinnamon?*

That afternoon, they sat under the metal bleachers near the edge of the field, peeling wrappers and watching the sky change shape above them.

"I knew you'd come back," Conor said, without looking at him. "You're not the kind of person who disappears for good."

"I didn't want to," Tristan admitted. "But sometimes you don't get to decide what disappears."

Conor tossed a pebble toward the field. "Then we'll decide what comes back."

"What if it doesn't come back the same?"

"Then we'll fix it," Conor said, and handed him another Pop Tart.

Tristan didn't respond. He was still trying to believe that.

He glanced down at his notebook—Miss Scarlett had given him a fresh one with blank pages and no expectations. On the first page, he wrote a single sentence: *Some people don't fall apart all at once—they unravel quietly.*

It wasn't a story yet. But it would be.

That evening, he lay in bed with the notebook beside him and the pencil still tucked behind his ear. The house was quiet. His mother was on the phone in the other room, laughing too loudly. His stepfather hadn't said more than three words to him all day. But for once, the silence didn't feel like an indictment. It felt like a space. A beginning.

He thought about Miss Scarlett's face when she read his short story aloud to him in the visitation room. The way her voice caught slightly at the end. He thought about Conor's ridiculous jokes, his refusal to let the space between them grow too wide.

And then, for the first time in a long time, he closed his eyes and whispered a single word.

Thanks.

Not to anyone in particular. Not for anything obvious. Just... thanks.

Thanks for a teacher who kept showing up.

Thanks for a friend who didn't ask for explanations.

Thanks for the part of him that still wanted to keep going.

He was almost asleep when he heard the sound. Distant. Unmistakable.

His mother's voice—angry, slurred, rising in a way it hadn't in months.

And then another voice. A man's. Not his stepfather's.

It was starting again.

Chapter 6

THE SEPARATION

*S*he used to tell him to find something, anything, to be grateful *for. Even when he didn't feel like it. Especially when he didn't feel like it. Gram said it was the only way to survive a world that couldn't always be trusted. He remembered the way her voice would catch slightly when she said it—as if she wasn't just passing on a lesson, but recalling one. One she'd lived. One she still lived. Today, in the waiting room, he tried. He closed his eyes, breathed slowly through his nose, and counted backward from five. When he opened them again, he stared at the gray laminate tile and whispered, "I'm grateful I know how to start over."*

A New State – Summer, 1992

A Fresh Start, Again

They moved again. This time to Pennsylvania.

Not far, just enough. Enough to reset the names and addresses and the tangled memories left behind in that neighboring state.

Enough for Tristan to rewrite the story, or at least to pretend it had already been rewritten. He'd gotten good at that—reshaping memory until it no longer cut.

He didn't miss the town they left. He didn't talk about it. Not with his mother, who seemed so relieved to escape it she practically floated into this new life. Not with Marie, who handled change like a girl already used to instability. And not with himself, which was easiest of all.

Sixth grade became a new draft. Clean margins. No footnotes. He stepped into the building with sharpened pencils and a mind like a sponge, ready to absorb anything but the truth. The lie had not disappeared—but it had dulled. Like something submerged underwater. He could still see its shape, but the edges were too blurry to define. And that, in its own way, was a kind of relief.

He joined the school play. Nothing too flashy, just a background role in the fall production. But he loved the cadence of rehearsals, the sacred hush backstage, the dimming lights and painted sets and how the right line at the right moment could hush a room. He liked being someone else, even for just a scene or two.

Academics came easily. They always had. He never flaunted it—he learned early that brilliance didn't win you friends, just suspicion. But he kept his grades steady, neat, correct. Enough to get noticed. Not enough to stand out.

Baseball, though—that was where he thrived.

There was something about the precision of it. The stillness before the pitch, the sudden violence of contact, the silence afterward. He could hit. He could run. He could turn a double play like he was born to do it. On the field, no one asked about his past. They only watched his feet, his hands, the quiet fire in his eyes when he caught a line drive.

That's where he met Phillip and Stewart.

Phillip was easy. Steady. A good listener. Always down for a sleepover or a two-hour campaign on some video game Tristan didn't even like that much. They invented stupid things together—like "knee football" in the basement and a fake superhero named Laser Cat. Phillip's parents were kind and attentive. They asked him about school, about theater, about books he was reading. They didn't pry. They just made room.

Stewart—*Stew*, as everyone called him—was different. Four years older and already in high school, he shouldn't have had time for a sixth grader. But somehow, they clicked. Stew was fast—on the field, in conversation, in his ability to read a room. He could dunk. He quoted Shakespeare and Tupac in the same breath. His home life was a mess—something Tristan understood intuitively, even if Stew never said it outright. But their connection ran deep. Unspoken. Mutual.

With them, he didn't have to explain himself. Not the flash of anger that came when things felt too tight. Not the blank stares when someone asked where he used to live. Not the strange detachment that crept in sometimes when adults got too nice. They didn't need to know everything. They just let him be.

"You ever think about moving again," Phillip asked once as they packed up after practice.

Tristan shrugged. "Only if I have to."

"What's that mean?" Stew said, tossing the ball into his glove without looking.

"Means some things move without asking you first," Tristan replied, and Stew didn't press.

They just walked off the field together, the conversation swallowed by the sound of gravel under their cleats.

By winter, he started to believe that maybe this was how things stayed. That maybe the lie, the pain, the jagged pieces of his earlier life, could finally lie dormant beneath this snow-covered Pennsylvania quiet.

It wasn't healing.

But it was peace.

And for now, that was enough.

The Quiet Fracture

Seventh grade arrived with a strange kind of confidence. Not the loud kind. Not the kind that drew eyes or changed how he walked down the hall. Just a soft, inner knowing that he could handle it. That school was something he could win at, if he chose to. And he did.

He and Marie were in the same building now. It made things feel more stable somehow, like there was someone else navigating the weird in-between of adolescence with him. They didn't talk much about their past, and definitely not about the move. But sometimes they'd exchange a glance when someone mentioned families, or a group of parents clapped too enthusiastically from the back of the auditorium. They understood things that other kids didn't. That kind of understanding didn't need language.

The year moved quickly. Tristan got cast in a larger role in the spring play. He nailed his monologues. People clapped. Teachers pulled him aside after class to compliment his performance. He smiled and thanked them, but he never lingered too long in the attention. It was a currency he didn't trust. Applause was loud and short-lived. He preferred consistency—routines, rehearsals, schedules he could depend on.

Phillip was still his anchor. Their friendship deepened. Weekends were a blur of video games, baseball practice, and entire conversations held in code or inside jokes. Stewart, though older, remained a steady presence. He'd started driving and sometimes picked Tristan up just to shoot hoops or grab food and talk about everything that didn't matter, which was their code for talking about everything that did.

At school, Tristan was thriving. Teachers called him dependable, curious, respectful. He was, in many ways, the student every teacher hoped to have. But no one saw how carefully he constructed that persona. No one noticed the way he sidestepped questions about family vacations or avoided writing essays about home. He was a master at leaving things out.

At home, the foundation was starting to shift.

It was small at first. His mother was out more often. At first it was errands, then book clubs, then some vague "meeting" with friends she never named.

"You're out a lot lately," he said once, not looking up from his homework.

"I have things I need to do," she replied quickly.

"For work?"

"For me," she said, and kissed the top of his head like that made it better.

His stepfather tried to hold the house together, but something in his spirit had begun to unravel. The dinners were quieter. The smiles more forced. Marie noticed it, too. She stopped bringing friends over.

Still, Tristan pretended not to see it. He built his days with precision—morning routines, school, homework, theater, baseball, sleepovers. If the house felt different, he'd simply stay out of it longer. If his mother felt distant, he'd find her in the applause at the end of a scene or the slap of the ball in his glove.

He never let the cracks show. Not at school. Not with his friends. Not even with himself.

By spring, his mother was gone more nights than not.

Still, he told himself it was nothing. Just another version of change. Another way to adjust.

That's what he was best at, after all.

The Summer Collapse

The summer after seventh grade was supposed to be predictable. That was the whole point.

He would go to Conor's house like he always did, spend a week playing street hockey and eating peanut butter sandwiches and watching reruns of old game shows they could recite word-for-word. Conor's family still lived in the same home—the one with the creaky screen door and the slanted back porch—and that sameness was something Tristan had come to count on. It was one of the only constants left.

He never told Conor everything. Just the bits that made sense, the ones that didn't disturb the rhythm. They'd become best friends back in fifth grade before everything spiraled again, and Conor had never asked too many questions about where he'd gone or why. He was just happy when Tristan came back. That was enough.

It was midweek when the call came.

His mother's voice was cheerful, oddly so. She told him they were moving—again. That she and Marie had already packed most of their things and had found a new place, just a neighborhood over. His stepfather wouldn't be coming.

"Why didn't you wait until I got home?" he asked, gripping the phone tighter.

"It was time," she said. "We need to get started."

"Started with what?"

"A new chapter," she answered, like it was a line she'd practiced.

There was no anger in her tone, just a kind of clean finality, like she was reading from a script.

He felt the floor tilt slightly beneath him.

She said it was for the best. That things hadn't been working. That they'd still see him, of course, and figure everything out once he got back. But even as she said it, he could hear something brittle behind her voice.

Tristan didn't ask questions. He didn't even blink.

He hung up the phone and returned to the living room, sat beside Conor, and picked up his controller. They played two more rounds of Mario Kart. He didn't lose once.

It wasn't until later that week, when he returned to Pennsylvania, that the truth snapped fully into view. His mother had moved out. She'd taken Marie and a few suitcases and signed the lease on a tired two-bedroom house that smelled faintly of mildew and new paint. His stepfather hadn't just been left, he'd been gutted. And when Tristan asked if there had been someone else, his mother said only, "Things happen." She didn't deny it. She didn't confirm it either.

"Is he the reason?" Tristan asked quietly.

She paused long enough for him to know the answer, even before she spoke.

"Life's complicated," she said.

"Doesn't have to be," he muttered, but she was already walking away.

But he knew.

The man she'd left for was younger. Handsome. Always around now.

And just like that, the image he had clung to—of her as unbreakable, untouchable, righteous in her decisions—shattered.

For years, he'd told himself she was the one thing he could always count on. That she had saved him from the hospital, from Peter, from the burning wreckage of a childhood that never got off the ground. But now that story didn't quite hold.

And the lie—*the* lie—breathed again. Subtle but persistent.

Peter had never come after him. Never pushed for visits or phone calls. Never showed up to reclaim the son taken from him. Still, there was a piece of Tristan that remembered the warmth of his arms, the steady way he used to say his name, the way his presence had filled a room without raising his voice.

Tristan didn't let himself wonder what life would've been like if he'd stayed with Peter. But the wondering was there. Always beneath the surface.

So he did what he always did. He adjusted.

He unpacked his bags. Memorized the layout of this new rental. Learned how the windows stuck when you opened them. Noted which cabinet held the cereal and which faucet sputtered before it flowed.

And he kept the fire buried. Not extinguished. Just tucked beneath layers of planning and performance and perfection.

The trick, he reminded himself, was to never let it flicker too high. To stay in control. To never need more than what he could manufacture himself.

The Slow Unraveling

The move hadn't taken them far—just a neighborhood away—but everything felt different.

His mother seemed relieved, like she'd finally exhaled after holding her breath for years. The house was smaller, colder. There were no framed photos in the hallway, no lingering smell of dinner by the time Tristan got home from school. Just a couch, a television, and the low thrum of silence. She let him and Marie do what they wanted. No curfews. No rules. No questions.

At first, it felt like freedom.

Eighth grade brought with it a fresh schedule and new teachers, but it lacked the novelty of the year before. The routines were familiar now. Wake, dress, pretend. Perform at school. Stay awake too late. Sleep with one eye open.

Tristan still did well—academically, socially, on the field. He was too proud to let his grades slip. He cared too much about how he was perceived, about keeping the image intact. But cracks were forming. Quiet ones.

He started skipping breakfast. Stayed up until 2 a.m. on school nights watching late-night reruns of shows he didn't care about. He didn't rebel outwardly—there were no tantrums or outbursts—but something inside him was growing numb.

Marie started drifting, too. She spent more time at friends' houses. Came home with stories Tristan couldn't verify. Their conversations thinned. They shared a roof but lived parallel lives. He tried not to think about the nights she didn't come home until morning.

His stepfather, still living nearby, tried to stay connected. He'd drop off groceries once in a while or take them to dinner when his mother remembered to coordinate. Tristan appreciated him, quietly. But the bond they had been building before the separation now hung in limbo—half-formed, awkward, unfinished.

And then there was the man.

The younger one. The one his mother had chosen.

He was around more often now. His presence was casual, but invasive. He cracked jokes Tristan didn't find funny. He opened the fridge like it belonged to him. Sometimes, late at night, Tristan heard his voice down the hall and clenched his fists without knowing why.

Once, he caught the man in the kitchen after midnight.

"You hungry, kid?" the man asked, rummaging through the fridge.

"Not for anything here," Tristan replied, and went back to his room before the man could answer.

Tristan never asked questions. He didn't confront. But his mind worked overtime, weaving and unweaving stories, trying to make sense of it all. And beneath that quiet hum, the old fire flickered again—reminding him that something had once burned so hot it nearly consumed him.

He hadn't spoken Peter's name in years. But sometimes, in the dark, he wondered what would've happened if he had just told the truth. If he had let Peter stay. If he had fought for something real before it all was stripped away.

But eighth grade wasn't for wrestling with the past.

It was for survival. Image. Control.

So, he played the game. Said the right things. Got straight A's. Performed in the winter showcase. Helped Phillip build a science fair project that won regionals. Stayed late after practice to run drills no one asked him to.

The lie remained untouched. The grief, unspoken.

But his body remembered. His spirit remembered.

And something—though he couldn't yet name it—was quietly unraveling.

Love, Fire and the Fight

Ninth grade began with a surge of momentum.

New school. Bigger campus. Older students. New pressures. He was ready for it—or at least, he had convinced himself that he was. It felt like a new stage, and if there was one thing Tristan had mastered, it was how to play a part.

He joined student council. Tried out for the baseball team again and made varsity. Excelled in English, especially when they covered dramatic literature. There was something about slipping into a character that made everything inside him sit still for a while. Teachers loved him. Coaches praised him. But none of it touched the growing ache beneath his ribs.

Then came the girl.

A senior. Beautiful. Confident. She saw him in the hallway one morning, and for reasons he couldn't explain, she started talking to him. And he didn't run. She was magnetic, and Tristan fell hard, fast, and completely.

It wasn't just infatuation. It was something else. Something that made him feel important, adult, chosen. She laughed at his jokes, told him he was brilliant, kissed him like she meant it.

"Why me?" he asked once, the words slipping out before he could stop them.

She grinned. "Because you look like you're thinking about five things at once, and I want to know what they are."

"You might not like them," he said.

"I'll take my chances."

Being with her made the chaos at home shrink, if only for a moment.

He started spending more time away from the house. His mother noticed but said nothing. She was preoccupied—still involved with the same man she had left his stepfather for. They weren't subtle about it anymore. The man came and went like he belonged there, and Tristan had long stopped pretending not to notice.

He hated him.

He hated the way he laughed. The way he talked to Marie like she was his. The way he looked at his mother, casually, as if none of the damage mattered.

And then came the moment he couldn't unsee.

It was a Saturday morning. Tristan had come home early from a friend's house. The front door was unlocked. He walked in and found them in the kitchen—his mother and the man, in a moment that confirmed everything he had suspected.

Something inside him cracked.

The room blurred. He charged.

He didn't think. Didn't weigh the consequences. Didn't measure the optics. He just moved—rage first, fists clenched, heart pounding with years of confusion and betrayal.

There was yelling. A crash. His mother screamed.

And then, the sirens.

The police came. Neighbors stood in doorways, watching as Tristan was led out in handcuffs, his cheeks flushed with shame and fury. His mother was on the lawn, barefoot, arms crossed, speaking in low, rapid tones to one of the officers. He didn't look at her.

They held him at the station for hours. Eventually, his stepfather came. He signed a paper. Spoke softly to the officers. Said things like *"He's a good kid, he just lost it for a second."*

"Did you?" his stepfather asked quietly once they were alone.

"Lose it?" Tristan said.

"Yeah."

Tristan stared at the floor. "No. I just finally caught up."

There were talks of consequences. Charges. Counseling. Another hospital, maybe. His mother's suggestion, of course.

But it never happened.

Because someone else stepped in.

Gram.

She called Conor's parents. Said Tristan needed a place to stay—just for a while. Said he needed calm, familiarity, a space where he wouldn't feel like he had to perform. They said yes without hesitation.

The plan was simple: once the school year ended, he'd go spend a month with Conor, and during that time, his parents would figure out custody, housing, what came next.

The Summer They Never Came

He packed light. Just a duffel bag, his glove, and the quiet hope that this, like everything else in his life, would be temporary. His mother said it would be only a few weeks—just enough time for her and his stepfather to talk things through, figure out custody, settle into something resembling a plan. He didn't ask for details. He never did anymore. He had learned early that questions rarely led to truth. So he nodded, slung the bag over his shoulder, and climbed into the back seat of his stepfather's car as they drove him to Conor's house.

At first, it didn't feel like exile. It felt familiar. Comforting. A return to something that once held him when everything else was falling apart. Conor's family welcomed him without hesitation. His old room still smelled like it had in fifth grade—of pine and dryer sheets and boyhood simplicity. The creaky drawer in the desk still stuck, and the upstairs fan still clicked on every third rotation. Nothing had changed, and that sameness steadied him. He slept in late. Ate toaster waffles with powdered sugar. Played street hockey until dusk and drank too much soda. He and Conor laughed until their ribs hurt. They didn't talk about the fight. Conor didn't ask. And Tristan didn't offer anything.

One night, lying in the dark, Conor said, "You think she'll come?"

"She's my mom," Tristan answered.

"That's not what I asked."

Tristan rolled over. "Yeah. She'll come."

But he kept his eyes open until morning.

The first week passed without contact. Then two. His duffel bag stayed zipped at the foot of the bed, not out of laziness but as a quiet declaration to himself that this wasn't permanent. He was just visiting. Just waiting. The days bled together in a haze of sun and video games and grocery store trips with Conor's mom, who smiled at him with maternal warmth but never overstepped. When July turned to August and school supply lists began appearing in every aisle, the silence from his parents began to take on weight. At first, he left voicemails—calm, measured, polite. Just checking in. Just wondering when he might be picked up. No response. His mother's voicemail eventually filled. His stepfather never answered.

By mid-August, the duffel bag was no longer a symbol of hope—it was an accusation. A quiet reminder that no one had come for him. Not once. Not even to ask if he was okay.

He stopped calling.

Stopped waiting.

And yet, something in him refused to fully accept it. At night, he lay awake staring at the ceiling, imagining the sound of tires on gravel, the quick knock on the door, his mother's voice calling up the stairs. He would see her standing there, a weak apology in her eyes, and he would pretend not to care how long it had taken. But the knock never came. The driveway stayed empty. And each day that passed carved the truth deeper into his chest—this wasn't temporary. It wasn't a misunderstanding. It was a decision.

They had left him.

Not with anger. Not even with explanation. Just a silent, clean absence. The kind that doesn't announce itself but echoes all the louder because of it.

When Gram called and said she would handle the school paperwork, he barely responded. She said she had spoken with Conor's parents and arranged for him to stay permanently—at least for now. There was no talk of next steps. No mention of his mother or stepfather. Just gentle affirmation that he was safe. That everything would be okay.

Safe.

He wasn't even sure what that meant anymore. Safety had once been a hug from his mother, the weight of her hand on his back as she sang to him through tears. It had been Peter's deep voice reading bedtime stories and the heavy warmth of his arms wrapped around Tristan's small frame. Now it was the absence of chaos. The kindness of people who weren't obligated to love him but chose to anyway. Still, it didn't soothe the wound. Not this one.

He had spent the last four years rebuilding his life piece by piece—school, baseball, theater, grades, friends. He had played the part of the son worth keeping. The student worth praising. The kid who never asked for too much, never revealed too much, never made anyone uncomfortable. He had earned his place in this world by being easy to love and easier to forget.

And still—his mother had walked away.

He hadn't done anything wrong. That's what stung the most. He had tried so hard. Buried the lie. Hid the fire. Smiled when he was supposed to. He had played the long game, trusting that if he became the best version of what they wanted, they would never let him go again.

But now they had.

He realized then that his entire life had been built on the fragile hope that love was something you could earn. That if you did everything right, people would stay. That if you hid the worst parts of yourself deep enough, long enough, no one would leave.

But they had.

And the boy who had once sobbed in the back of a police car, who had lied to protect the mother he adored, who had longed for Peter but swallowed that grief whole, now understood what it meant to be truly, completely alone. The abandonment wasn't loud. It was quiet. Administrative. The absence of a phone call. The silence between school years. The choice to never look back.

So when the first day of school arrived and Conor's mom handed him a packed lunch and his new class schedule, he smiled and thanked her. Walked through the doors of that new year like a shadow of the boy he used to be. He would play the part again. He always did.

But something essential had broken.

Something deep and quiet and real.

And from that day on, he would carry the unspoken truth that the people who gave him life had let him go—again.

And this time, it was permanent.

Chapter 7

THE GATSBY ERA

He had learned not to expect much from people. But Gram still told him to be grateful. For kindness. For quiet. For the chance to start again.

In the waiting room, he reached for that. Not with urgency—those days were gone—but with a calm kind of ache that only comes after disappointment has settled in and made itself a guest. He sat still, thumb tracing a slow circle against the grain of the wooden bench, and whispered, "I'm grateful for the ones who chose me when they didn't have to."

The light buzzed above him. He didn't look up. Something about this place made you stop needing to. The clock, if there was one, didn't matter anymore.

Reinvention – Fall, 1995

By the time August faded into September, Maryland had already begun to feel like a stage set. A blank backdrop, waiting for the character he would become. Tristan wasn't the boy who had arrived in fifth grade, broken and confused, or even the one who had walked into Conor's house with a bruised heart and a zipped duffel bag. He was fifteen now. Ten feet tall in a new high school. No parents hovering. No history following him from class to class. He was free—though it didn't feel like freedom. It felt like necessity.

Conor's family—kind, predictable, quietly affectionate— gave him rules, space, and breakfast. He didn't talk much to them beyond pleasantries, but there was stability there. No fights. No slammed doors. No strangers coming and going. Just Conor, who still made him laugh, and a quiet room upstairs that held the echo of childhood without demanding anything back.

He walked into his new school with a plan. Reinvention wouldn't be a defense mechanism this time—it would be a craft. He carried himself with ease. Offered answers without showing off. Joined clubs before they could ask questions. Theater. Debate. Baseball. Each one gave him a different mask to wear. Each one gave him something to control.

Once, after debate club, Conor caught him alone in the hall-way. "You're not actually like that with me," he said, half teasing.

"Like what?" Tristan asked, tightening his grip on the strap of his bag.

"All… put together. Like you know every answer before the question."

Tristan smirked. "Maybe I just like you better when you don't know the script."

Conor laughed, but his eyes lingered, as if he'd just stumbled onto a truth Tristan had no intention of admitting.

It didn't take long. Within weeks, teachers were praising him. Coaches were pulling him aside. Girls started to notice. He was funny. Confident. Kind. A little mysterious. He had learned the art of giving just enough—of keeping the real parts buried beneath charisma and charm. He wasn't faking it. He was curating it.

And then, in November, he met Jacob.

It was basketball season. Tristan wasn't on the team—too small, too late to try out—but Conor was, and Jacob was a senior captain. Jacob noticed Tristan watching from the sidelines after school and offered him a ride home. Nothing special. Just a casual kindness. But Tristan remembered it.

In the car, Jacob drummed his fingers on the steering wheel in time with the radio. "You play?" he asked, nodding toward the gym bag at Tristan's feet.

"Baseball," Tristan said.

"Figures, you've got that… don't-need-a-team-to-shine vibe."

Tristan frowned, unsure if it was a compliment or a read.

Jacob glanced over, grinning. "Not with me. Not with Him, either." He nodded upward like it was an invitation, not a command.

They talked. About plays. About God. About music and the ache of growing up too fast. Jacob didn't push. He just asked real questions—and listened. Slowly, he started bringing Tristan to church. Not the kind with pews and guilt and sermons that pressed down like stone—but a church that felt like breath. Music loud enough to drown out the static. People who sang like they meant it. Jacob's friends didn't look at him with pity. They didn't ask about his past. They just pulled him in like he belonged.

At first, Tristan stayed on the edges. He didn't know how to believe in something he couldn't touch. But something in the way Jacob spoke about Jesus—gentle, personal, sure—cut through the noise. Not religion. Not rules. Just a kind of love that didn't have to be earned.

It made him uneasy—how easy it seemed. Love without conditions always came with fine print, he thought. He didn't trust the absence of it. And yet, he kept showing up, as if repetition might prove it was real.

And that shook something loose in him.

He didn't say it out loud. Didn't pray any perfect prayers. But one night, after a youth service, he sat alone in his room and whispered something barely audible. Not a confession. Not even a request. Just: *"If you're real, I want to know you."*

And somehow, the room felt less empty after that.

They used to say time healed all wounds. Gram never believed that. She said time just covered them in new responsibilities and old distractions. The wound, she told him, was always there—quiet, pulsing, waiting for silence. For stillness.

In the waiting room, it pulsed.

A dull ache in his chest. Not grief. Not rage. Something quieter than both. A hairline fracture no one could see, but that he felt every time he sat still long enough to listen.

He shifted slightly on the bench. Closed his eyes.

"I'm grateful I can still feel it."

The Unexpected Rift

By the end of sophomore year, he had come to see Conor's house not as a temporary placement, but as home. It wasn't just the familiarity of the rooms or the predictable cadence of dinner and sleep. It was the rhythm of safety, the quiet reliability of knowing where the cereal went, which drawer held the spoons, when the front door would creak open at the end of the day. Conor's parents never said they loved him, not in words. But they made room for him—in their schedules, in their routines, in the ordinary spaces where real life lives. And he, for his part, had tried to earn it. Had studied hard. Smiled often. Washed his dishes without being asked. He wanted to be easy. Wanted to be worth the grace that had been given to him. And in that quiet effort, he had started to believe he belonged.

One night at dinner, Conor's dad asked if he had everything he needed for an upcoming project.

"Year," Tristan said, nodding quickly.

"You sure?"

"Positive."

The truth was he didn't even know what the project required. But needing something felt dangerous—like giving people a reason to reconsider keeping him.

It was the same spring that his faith began to deepen. Slowly. Quietly. Jacob had continued to mentor him—driving him to youth group, handing him dog-eared pages of scripture, leaving voicemails with prayers that lingered long after the phone calls ended. Church had become something real, not performative. Not obligatory. He found himself humming worship lyrics under his breath at practice. He started whispering prayers at night, not always sure who was listening, but needing to speak them anyway. There were even moments—brief but bright—when he believed that his story might finally be changing. That he wasn't just surviving. He was healing.

So when the conversation came—when Conor's parents, in hushed tones and kind smiles, told him they didn't think next year would be possible—it hit him like a blow to the chest. There was no malice in their eyes. No anger in their tone. But the message was clear. It was time to move on. He thanked them. Nodded. Said all the right things. And then went upstairs and curled into the corner of his bed like a boy who'd just been orphaned all over again. He couldn't cry. Couldn't scream. He just stared at the ceiling and thought, *why does this always happen?*

The lie roared back. The old one. The one with smoke and sirens and a boy too afraid to tell the truth. It didn't matter how well he behaved. How hard he tried. The end result was always the same: he would be left.

He wondered if it was some unspoken rhythm—how long people could carry him before the weight became too much. Maybe it was built into the clock of every relationship: kindness at first, strain in the middle, departure at the end.

It was Jessica who noticed first. They'd become close that year, sitting beside each other in math class, trading jokes and poems and inside glances across the cafeteria. She saw what no one else did—the quiet in his eyes, the tension in his shoulders, the way he smiled a little too quickly when someone asked how he was doing. And one day, halfway through a lecture, she slid a folded note across his desk that said: *If you ever need somewhere else to go, I already talked to my parents. We have room.*

At first, he didn't believe her. He read it twice. Thought it was a joke. But that night, when he called Gram and told her what had happened—how he was being asked to leave, again—Gram didn't question it. She just grew quiet and said she'd follow up. Within two days, Jessica confirmed it. Her parents had opened their home. And so, a few weeks later, with nothing but his duffel bag and a heart full of silence, he moved again.

Gram called that night. "You doing okay, sweetheart?"

"I'm fine."

She paused long enough for him to know she didn't believe him. "You don't have to be fine to be mine."

He almost said thank you. Instead, he stared at the ceiling and let the words settle like something he might believe someday.

Jessica's family was kind. Warm in a way that didn't feel performative. Her mother left folded towels on his bed. Her father talked to him like he mattered. They never asked for his story. They just made space for him to write a new one. And he was grateful. Deeply, desperately grateful. But still, it didn't erase the ache.

He never said it out loud, but losing Conor's family broke something in him. The kind of break that doesn't scream, but simmers. The kind that seeps into your bones and makes you question whether belonging is something you're ever allowed to trust.

Even now, sitting in the waiting room, fingers tracing slow circles into the wooden bench, he could still feel the sting of it. Of being chosen, then unchosen. Of trying his hardest and still coming up short. Of being handed kindness and not knowing how to hold it without breaking it in two.

And somewhere beneath the silence, the shame whispered again: *It's your fault.*

The room was quiet again. That thick, padded kind of quiet— like a theater after the lights have come up but no one's stood yet. He shifted slightly in the chair. The cushion squeaked beneath him, but no one looked up. There was no clock on the wall. No way to know how long he'd been sitting there. Long enough to forget what it felt like to be expected somewhere.

He thought about the summer before junior year. The way the front door of Conor's house had clicked shut behind him without ceremony. No hugs. No tears. Just an ending wrapped in courtesy. That kind of goodbye left no bruises. But it bled just the same.

He wondered, not for the first time, if it would have been better to be thrown out. To be yelled at. Blamed. At least then, he would've known what to fix. But silence? Silence stayed. It curled up in the folds of your memory and whispered things like you were too much. You were always too much.

He clenched his jaw and let out a breath he hadn't realized he was holding. And then, barely audible, just above the hum of the air vent, he whispered: "I'm grateful I still remember what it felt like to be chosen. Even if only for a while."

The Quiet Rescue

He hadn't seen it coming. Not really.

Conor's house had become his blueprint for stability. The place he imagined he'd return to on college breaks. The family he thought might someday call him their own. He didn't know what shifted, only that something had. It started small— too many late arrivals, too many quiet dinners. The hallway felt tighter. The silences longer. He sensed their compassion straining, like a shelf bearing too much weight.

Tristan had worked hard to be light. Polite. Easy. He kept his grades perfect, took the trash out without being asked, stayed in his room when he needed to scream. He thought he'd done enough. That this time, finally, he wouldn't be too much.

But even in a good home, even with good people, sometimes you could still wear out your welcome.

It broke something in him.

Not all at once. Not loud. Just a quiet fraying. The realization that even the places that feel safest can still let you go.

It was Jessica who caught him.

They'd been friends all year—seatmates in math class, partners for presentations, hallway confidants in the in-between moments when the world went still enough for truth to sneak through. She was quiet but not timid. Observant in a way that made people uncomfortable if they had something to hide. She never asked about his past. She didn't need to. She saw it in the way he flinched when doors closed too quickly, in the way his eyes scanned rooms before he entered them.

They were graphing exponential functions when she said it.

"If you need somewhere to go next year," she murmured, eyes still on her notebook, "my parents said it's okay."

He blinked. "What?"

"My house," she said, as if they'd been talking about it for days. "You can stay. I already asked them. They've got the extra room."

He didn't know what to say.

That night, he sat in the closet of Conor's guest room with the light off, knees pulled to his chest, listening to the house he loved breathing above him. He whispered the whole story to Gram in a broken call that lasted under three minutes. She didn't offer advice. Just sat in silence on the other end and said she would handle it.

Two days later, Jessica confirmed it was settled. Her parents had agreed.

The day he left Conor's house, no one cried. No one fought. There was no moment of closure. Just a quiet ride, his duffel bag in the back seat, his chest feeling like something had been scooped out of it and left unstitched.

Jessica's family welcomed him with the same quiet grace she had always shown. Her mother made blueberry pancakes the first morning and called him sweetie without hesitating. Her father handed him a house key by dinner and said, "No rush to figure things out." They didn't ask him to earn his keep. They just kept the lights on.

And that—more than the food, the room, the clean towels folded like hotel linens—was what undid him.

They expected nothing.

They just chose him.

He slept lightly for the first week, afraid to settle in. He kept his bag packed just in case. But Jessica never treated him like a guest. She let him be quiet. Let him disappear into his music or his books without apology. She didn't try to fix him. Just made space.

"Safe isn't the same as alive," she told him once, after finding him staring out the window for an hour.

He looked at her, almost smiling. "Maybe alive is overrated."

It was the first time he realized how powerful that was.

Space.

Not to explain. Not to justify. Just to exist.

And still—he grieved.

He missed Conor's house. Not for what it was, but for what it had almost been. For the fantasy of permanence it had given him. For the belief that maybe, just maybe, he wouldn't be passed along again.

Even now, years later, seated in the sterile stillness of the waiting room, the ache lingered. Conor had never said goodbye. Neither had his parents. He wondered sometimes if they ever thought of him. If they ever regretted it.

When he tried to picture their faces, the memory felt like a photograph left too long in the sun—faded, edges curling inward. It was easier to remember the door than the people behind it.

But mostly, he just tried not to remember the sound of the door clicking shut behind him without anyone watching.

The Year of Almost

By the end of junior year, the seams were starting to strain again. Jessica's family never said anything harsh, but he could sense the discomfort—the long pauses at dinner when he got home late, the hesitant glances between her parents when he shut down in conversation. He had worked so hard to become this version of himself, and still, it was never quite enough.

One night, Jessica's dad lingered in the doorway after dinner. "You've been quiet lately," he said gently.

Tristan forced a smile. "Just tired."

"Don't work so hard at being tired."

The comment was light, but Tristan caught the edge of it. He wondered if this was how ending began—with sentences no one meant as warnings.

He wasn't disruptive. But he was heavy. His moods unpredictable. His silences too long. The emotional weight he carried bled through the cracks no matter how carefully he tried to patch them.

Then, in a twist Tristan hadn't expected, it was Jacob who helped find the next chapter.

Jacob had graduated, but they still spoke. When things started unraveling at Jessica's, it was Jacob who reached out to a family from his church, the Gallos. A quiet, kind couple with three grown kids and an open heart for taking in strays like Tristan. They didn't hesitate. They just opened their door and said, "Stay as long as you need."

So senior year began with another move. Another new room. Another set of expectations to navigate. But this time, it felt different. The Gallos didn't ask for anything extraordinary. They didn't hover or offer therapy sessions at dinner. They just loved him in the simplest, most consistent way he had ever known. Meals were shared. Chores were expected. Trust was given freely.

Once, after dinner, Mrs. Gallo caught him washing dishes before she could. "You don't have to earn your keep here," she said.

"I know," he replied, keeping his eyes on the plate in his hands.

She touched his shoulder lightly. "Then why do you look like you're afraid to stop?"

For the first time in years, Tristan felt like he could breathe without apologizing for taking up space.

He flourished.

Varsity soccer and baseball became outlets for energy he once spent hiding. He carried a weighted course load and still managed to lead chapel announcements, star in the fall play, and volunteer with the youth group. Teachers praised him. Peers looked up to him. Parents at church whispered to the Gallos that they'd never met such a respectful, mature young man.

But even then, something in him remained locked. There were days when he stared out the window of his AP English class, wondering if this perfect image he had created would ever feel like home. There were nights when he lay in bed, hands folded behind his head, asking God to remove the ache that pulsed under all the achievement. The lie hadn't vanished. It had only grown more subtle—woven into the way he avoided questions, the way he couldn't look at photos of Peter without his stomach tightening. The fire still lived in him. But now, it burned clean and quiet, like coals beneath polished wood.

Jocelyn had transferred again for senior year, this time back to her original school. But they kept in touch. Long emails. Occasional calls. One night in early spring, she visited for a school performance. They sat on a bench afterward, quiet beneath the stars, and she looked at him with something fierce in her eyes.

"You're still hiding," she said.

"I'm not," he lied, gently.

She didn't argue. Just nodded slowly. And then she whispered, "You're still worth loving, even if you never tell anyone everything."

The words stayed with him longer after she'd gone—clinging like the smell of her perfume on his jacket.

They were almost unbearable in their generosity.

He wanted to hold her then. To explain everything. But he couldn't. So he just said thank you, and watched her disappear into the parking lot, knowing she was right.

That was the year it all came together—on paper, at least. His college acceptance gave him an early exit from the usual senior panic. His essays were brilliant. His interviews impeccable. He graduated with awards, scholarships, and offers that made guidance counselors beam with pride.

Gram came to the ceremony. Sat front row, clutched a tissue the whole time, and cried when he walked across the stage.

His mother didn't come.

He didn't expect her to.

But it still hurt.

After the ceremony, he posed for pictures with the Gallos and Gram, letting their joy cover the wound just long enough. He gave a speech that made people cry. He smiled for a hundred photos. He laughed when he didn't feel like laughing. Because he had learned how to make others feel safe even when he wasn't.

That night, after all the noise had faded, he sat on the backsteps of the Gallo home, staring at the stars. The ache came back. So he prayed—barely a whisper, really.

"God... I don't know what happens next. But please... don't let me lose myself."

It wasn't poetic. It wasn't desperate. It was just honest. And for the first time in a long time, it felt like maybe—just maybe—someone had heard him.

The Descent

College began the way all fresh starts do—wide-eyed, clean-swept, full of intention. Tristan stepped onto campus with a duffel bag, a laptop, and a curated smile that suggested he had it all figured out. He didn't. But he was exceptional at making people think he did. He had been accepted into one of the most prestigious universities in New England, and no one questioned whether he belonged. His professors praised his insight. His peers gravitated toward his charm. He held court without trying, folding himself seamlessly into every room. He joined clubs, made the dean's list, and racked up accolades that affirmed what he needed the world to believe—that he was thriving.

But beneath all the momentum, he was empty. The drive that carried him into each day was not joy or even ambition, but fear. Fear that the lie would catch up. Fear that someone would ask the right question. Fear that all the effort, all the curated perfection, would eventually crack and reveal the boy who was still bleeding beneath the mask. He couldn't name the moment it started to unravel—there wasn't a single collapse, no dramatic fall from grace. Just a slow, steady drift toward numbness. A few pills to stay up and study. A drink to ease the ache. Parties that blurred into each other. Hookups that meant nothing but distraction. He chased sensation, not connection. Anything to stay ahead of the emptiness.

A friend once asked if he ever got tired of pretending.

"Pretending what," he'd said.

"That everything's fine."

Tristan had laughed it off, but the question hung in the air for weeks, like a mirror he couldn't quite bring himself to look into.

He dated two women seriously in college—both brilliant, magnetic, broken in their own ways. The first made him feel invincible. She was wild, unpredictable, full of intensity. He mistook that for passion. They burned hot and fast, unraveling by winter. The second was quieter, more introspective, and devastatingly intuitive. She saw through his surface, saw the storm behind the smile, and tried to reach him. But he couldn't meet her there. Every time she got close, something in him recoiled, afraid to be seen, afraid to be held accountable to the tenderness he didn't know how to accept. That second breakup undid something in him. After that, he stopped trying to love anyone deeply. He flirted, charmed, disappeared. He stopped apologizing for it.

His faith became harder to access in those years—not because he stopped believing, but because he didn't know how to carry it while spiraling. He still believed Jesus was real. But he wasn't sure he was still welcome. He went to chapel services when he could muster the energy, sometimes sat in the back just to hear the music. Occasionally he'd journal scraps of prayers—pleas he couldn't quite finish. Mostly, he just stayed moving. Stillness hurt too much.

But there was one anchor that never slipped: Gram.

She called every morning. Even when he didn't answer, she left a message. Sometimes just scripture. Sometimes just a reminder to drink water or rest. And sometimes—on the days he needed it most without realizing why—she said the words he couldn't say to himself: "You are not too far gone." He visited her every chance he could, flying to Florida during breaks. Those visits were sacred. Simple. A quiet meal, a long walk, the warmth of her hands on his face as she told him how proud she was, not of his achievements, but of his heart. Of how he still tried, even when it hurt. She never asked about the relationships, the drugs, the slipping grades toward the end. She didn't need to. She just loved him.

Once, on a call after a particularly bad night, she said, "You sound tired in your bones, sweetheart."

He swallowed hard. "Just been busy."

"You can be busy and still be lost."

The words unsettled him, because he knew she was right—and because she didn't push him to admit it.

Without condition. Without fear.

Gram was the only woman Tristan ever truly felt safe with. And that truth haunted him. He didn't want to be emotionally detached. He didn't want intimacy to feel like danger. But after everything—his mother, the women he couldn't protect, the ones he couldn't trust—he had learned that distance was safer than surrender. Love, real love, asked for too much.

And so he performed. He smiled. He graduated on time. His resume was immaculate. His friendships wide and shallow. His heart a sealed vault of memories no one else had a key to. When he walked across the stage at graduation, no one could see the fracture lines. But they were there. And as he turned the tassel, Tristan knew one thing with absolute clarity: he had no idea who he really was anymore. He only knew he couldn't go home.

Home had become less a place and more a list of people he'd already lost.

New York was waiting. A new mask. A new life. One more chance to pretend he wasn't still bleeding.

Arrival

The city didn't welcome him. It consumed him. New York was

too loud, too fast, too full of people who didn't care who you were unless you had something they needed. Which made it perfect. Tristan arrived with a freshly pressed suit, an apartment he couldn't afford, and a position at one of the most prestigious consulting firms in Manhattan. He should have been thrilled. The boy who once lay curled up in a psych ward was now standing in a high-rise conference room, giving presentations to billionaires. But inside, he felt nothing. Or maybe too much. It was hard to tell anymore.

He moved through the city like a ghost in designer shoes. His days were filled with meetings and metrics. His nights with noise and numbing. Happy hours that turned into late nights. Women who saw the suit and the smile but never touched the soul beneath.

He told himself it was freedom—this endless carousel of names and faces—but the trust was uglier: anonymity was safer when you couldn't risk being known.

He kept his phone charged mostly for Gram. She still called every morning. Sometimes he answered. Sometimes he didn't. When he did, she never asked about the firm, or the skyline, or whether he was making friends. She asked if he was sleeping. If he was praying. If he was kind to himself.

He wasn't.

He called Jocelyn once. Just to hear her voice. She answered, softly, like she wasn't surprised. They talked about nothing for ten minutes. Weather. Books. A new coffee shop she loved. He didn't tell her he'd moved. Didn't ask how she was, not really. And when she asked how *he* was, he lied.

"Good," he said, too quickly. "Busy."

She was quiet for a beat. Then: "I hope you remember who you are."

He almost said, "I'm trying." But the words felt like they'd expose too much, so he let the silence do the lying for him.

He didn't know what to say to that. So, he changed the subject. And a minute later, the call ended.

He sat there for a long time after that, staring out at the lights of a city that didn't even know his name. It was beautiful, yes. But brutal. And even now, as the success he'd always imagined stretched out in front of him, he felt the ache of something missing. A longing that wealth and admiration couldn't touch. He had everything he'd once dreamed of—respect, prestige, anonymity. And yet, beneath the layers of polish, he was still the boy in the hospital, the boy who lied, the boy who never got picked up.

That's what haunted him most. Not the chaos. Not even the lie. But the abandonment. The memory of standing on the curb outside Conor's house that summer after ninth grade, waiting for a car that never came. It lived in his bones. It shaped how he walked into rooms. How he held people at arm's length. How he sabotaged love before it could disappoint him.

The city would never ask why—only what he could deliver. In some ways, that was the mercy he thought he wanted.

He never said it out loud, but he believed it—that the wound was his fault. That Peter suffered because of him. That love had conditions. And if he wasn't perfect, it would leave.

The city would love him for his brilliance. It would reward his detachment. He could keep the mask on here, maybe forever. But even as he told himself that, even as he stepped into the elevator and straightened his tie, he knew the ache wouldn't go away.

Not until he stopped running.

Chapter 8

CITY LIFE, PART 2

*G*ram always told him to breathe. Deep, steady, like waves smoothing the edges of something sharp. In the waiting room, he tried. But the memories were louder now. Sharper. This was the part he didn't talk about. The years when he almost forgot who he was. The part of the story that wrapped its hands around his throat and whispered, "This is all you'll ever be." He leaned forward, elbows on knees, and tried again. Inhale. Hold. Exhale. "I'm grateful I survived," he whispered. "Even though I'm still figuring out what that means."

The Descent Begins – Summer, 2006

He had believed for a while that he could be someone else. That if he just worked hard enough, dressed sharp enough, smiled at the right people, said all the right things, maybe the boy who once lived in shadows could finally vanish. New York didn't just welcome that illusion. It rewarded it. The city made gods of men like him—brilliant, charming, tireless. He arrived the summer after graduation, diploma in one hand, job offer in the other, and the echoes of applause still ringing faintly in his ears. He told himself he was ready. Ready for the skyline. The suits. The long hours and longer nights. But what he really meant was, "I'm done looking back."

He moved into a studio apartment in midtown—just far enough from the noise to sleep, just close enough to pretend he didn't need peace. His company gave him a title he hadn't earned and a salary that made his chest tighten with both pride and fear. He rose early. Ran miles before the sun stretched over the skyline. Shaved with precision. Learned to knot a Windsor blindfolded. The city demanded performance, and he was good at the dance. Coffee by six. Emails by seven. Metrics.

Meetings. Praise. Repeat. Every day an exercise in reinvention.

Once, a senior partner pulled him aside in the hallways. "You've got the look," he said, half admiring, half warning.

"What look?" Tristan asked.

"The kind that makes people believe you've already won."

Tristan smiled as if it were praise, but the words trailed him back into the desk like a shadow.

But inside, he was unraveling.

The first few months passed in a blur of motion—so much movement he never had to sit still. Stillness, after all, meant remembering. And remembering meant pain. There were nights he found himself in bars without knowing how he got there, conversations he couldn't recall with women whose names he never asked. He wasn't cruel. He was just… gone. Absent behind the eyes. Charming in the moment, then vanished before dawn.

He told himself it was freedom. That this was adulthood. That every twenty-something in Manhattan was doing the same thing. But he knew better. The women he chased weren't distractions. They were stand-ins. Echoes of the one woman who had left too many times. Who had never really looked back.

And each time he left their apartments before dawn, he felt the same dull truth settle in: he was practicing how to leave before anyone could do it to him.

He was searching, again and again, for something that might feel like home.

But Gram still called every morning.

It didn't matter how late he'd stayed out or how groggy his voice sounded. She never scolded. She just asked about his day. About his heart. About his faith. "Remember who you are," she'd say, like a benediction. "And who loves you." He never told her the whole truth. That he hadn't been to church in over a year. That the Bible she gave him stayed closed beneath his socks. That he hadn't prayed—not really prayed—since the week he moved in. But her voice still steadied something in him. Even as he drifted, she tethered him.

And sometimes, late at night, after the high wore off and the room quieted, he'd reach for his phone and reread their texts. Not for advice. Just to remember that someone, somewhere, still saw him.

Still believed he was more than the mask.

Still believed he was worth saving.

It scared him sometimes; how much he needed that belief to survive here. As if Gram's voice was the last thread holding him over the drop.

The truth was, Tristan knew exactly what he was doing.

By the end of that first year in the city, he had mastered the look—clean-cut, sharp, just enough undone to be envied. The firm loved him. Clients praised him. Recruiters hovered like vultures, impressed by the effortless way he carried both data and charm in the same breath. He could walk into a room and hold attention like it was his birthright. And for a while, that was enough.

Until it wasn't.

The compliment high faded faster each week, and in the quiet afterward he could hear the tick of something he couldn't outrun—like a metronome set to a life he hadn't chosen.

There was something missing in the silence. When the meetings ended, and the applause faded, and the spreadsheets were closed, he could hear it again. The ache. The memory. The fire he still dreamed about. Peter's name echoing through the smoke, the lie still tucked beneath his ribs, like a secret he wasn't brave enough to tell. And every time the loneliness returned, he found something new to bury it.

It started small. Just staying late. Grinding harder. Using the company gym, the company card, the company medication. The psychiatrist they sent him to prescribed Adderall without asking too many questions. "Performance anxiety," he'd said, scribbling a dosage on a pad before moving to the next topic.

"Will this make me better?" Tristan asked, half-joking.

"It will make you faster," the man replied, not looking up.

Faster felt close enough to better.

The pills made everything easier. Cleaner. Faster. More detached. He could stay up all night running models, get three hours of sleep, and still be charming by morning. And when that wasn't enough, there were always the clubs. Always the women.

They were never the same kind. Some were quiet. Some were loud. Some were older, some younger, some so desperate for something real that he almost hated himself for playing along. But none of them were Jocelyn. None of them knew how to read his eyes. None of them waited through his silence.

Jocelyn would have. And maybe that's why he avoided her. Waiting was an intimacy he wasn't ready to deserve.

And maybe that was the point. They wanted him for the image, for the Gatsby version he'd curated back in high school— the one that smiled on cue and always knew what to say. And he gave them what they asked for, over and over again, until he forgot what he looked like without the costume.

And underneath it all was the hole his mother left behind. He didn't name it that at the time, didn't admit it. But it was there. The absence. The betrayal. The unbearable truth that she never came back for him—not from Conor's, not from Jessica's, not even when he graduated college with honors and mailed her a photo she never acknowledged. Every time he thought he'd made peace with it, some random detail would bring it back. A mother and son laughing on the subway. A lullaby played on a violin in Central Park. An email from Gram, reminding him to be kind. To stay soft. To forgive.

He told himself these were coincidences. Then wondered why coincidences kept choosing him.

The pain wasn't constant. It just never left.

Gram was the one tether that held. She called every morning, as she always had through college. Asked him about his sleep, his spirit, his breath. He didn't always answer honestly, but he always picked up. Her voice grounded him, reminded him there was still one person in the world who had never walked away. She prayed for him out loud sometimes, even when he groaned and said,

"Gram, come on." And sometimes, when he hung up, he cried.

He learned to mute the phone before the tears came. New York tolerated brilliance, not breaking.

She never judged. Never pushed. But Tristan could hear the hope in her voice, the aching belief that the boy she loved was still somewhere inside him. That the God she spoke to every morning hadn't stopped chasing him. He wanted to believe that too. Some nights, he even prayed. Whispered into the dark, words that weren't quite sentences, longings that didn't have names. But the city was loud. And he was tired. And most days, the silence he craved felt too far away to find.

He still wrote to Jocelyn. Sometimes. A card at Christmas. A letter on her birthday. She always replied with words stitched with poetry and restraint. They talked about memories. About faith. About what they'd lost and maybe still hoped for. And slowly, a conversation opened up between them. By the time he turned twenty-seven, they had started talking again for real. Long phone calls, occasional video chats. There was laughter again. Wonder. And something else. Something quiet and old and tender. They were talking about seeing each other. About what it might mean to try again.

"Just don't lose yourself out there," she said on a late call, quiet enough that he had to lean into the receiver.

"I'll be fine," he answered.

"That's not what I asked."

Not with fanfare. Not with declarations. But with open hands. That's why he had come down on the train. That's what Kristen never knew. He wasn't just escaping the burnout or the emptiness. He was heading toward something. Toward someone. Jocelyn had agreed to meet him. To talk. To see if there was still something true between them.

But that conversation never happened.

The waiting room was different this time. Not because the walls had changed, or the magazines, or even the flickering light above the desk. But because something inside him had shifted.

There was a faint antiseptic tang he couldn't name, a rhythm under the hum that didn't belong to air vents. He told himself it was the building settling. He didn't look for the source.

Tristan sat still, elbows on his knees, head low, eyes not fixed on anything in particular. Just air. Just breath. It wasn't fear exactly. But it was something close to dread. The kind that makes your throat close up for no reason. The kind that says, "This is what dying feels like," even when your heart is still beating.

Gram would've said to give thanks. To whisper it into the ache. To remind his soul what was still true. But he couldn't find the words. Not this time. His hands were shaking. The air felt thick. And somewhere, under the noise, he heard the city again. That hum. That ache. The moment it all slipped past the point of return.

After the trip that never happened, things began to unravel quickly.

People started asking the easy questions— "You good?" "You sleeping?"—and he started giving the easy answers. The lies got lighter each time he told them.

It wasn't dramatic at first. Just a quiet kind of unspooling. The kind you don't notice until your days start blurring together and your nights feel longer than your weeks. He stopped calling people back. Stopped answering Jocelyn's messages. He told himself he was busy, that the project at work had grown, that Kristen—who had become something between a roommate and a temptation—was keeping him distracted. But that wasn't the truth. The truth was, Tristan was slipping. And somewhere deep inside, he knew it.

There was a moment in early spring when he found himself staring into the mirror of a hotel bathroom in SoHo after three straight nights of no sleep and too many pills to count. His eyes were bloodshot, his shirt wrinkled, his hands trembling as he tried to fix a tie he didn't even remember putting on. He'd been at a party. Or a fundraiser. Or maybe both. He wasn't sure anymore. He looked older in that mirror. Not wiser. Just more tired. More frayed.

He practiced a smile and watched it fail to reach his eyes. For a second he didn't recognize the man pretending to be him.

The boy with the chapel speech and varsity jacket was long gone. So was the man who once whispered prayers in the dark. What remained was a shell. A machine. A ghost who smiled for clients and collapsed in silence when no one was watching.

Work still praised him. The numbers never lied. He closed deals. Crushed forecasts. Delivered pitches that made boardrooms go silent. But inside, he was empty. The drugs helped—until they didn't. The women distracted him—until they didn't. And Kristen, lovely and damaged in her own way, became a mirror he hated looking into. She knew he was unraveling. Knew he was using her. But she didn't stop him. Maybe because she was unraveling too. Maybe because she saw herself in his undoing.

He tried to stop once. Threw the pills away. Stayed in one weekend. Read the letters Jocelyn had sent him and even opened his Bible again. It had dust on it, which felt poetic and cruel. He read Psalm 32 and underlined the part about groaning all day long.

"If You're still here, say something I can carry," he whispered, surprised by how small his voice sounded in his own apartment.

He thought of Gram and her soft voice, the way she always said Scripture wasn't just truth—it was invitation. He wanted to believe that. He wanted to believe he wasn't too far gone.

But by Monday, he was back at his desk, double dosing just to make it through a meeting with the senior partners. And by Tuesday, he was calling a guy he shouldn't have had in his contacts in the first place.

The dreams came next. Not the normal kind. Not even nightmares, exactly. Just flashes. Fire. Smoke. Peter's voice. A boy's face staring back at him with wide, wet eyes.

Sometimes another voice threaded through them—Jocelyn's, older now, steady: Don't lose yourself out there. He kept waking before he could promise he wouldn't.

A voice saying, "I didn't mean to." And sometimes, a whisper. "You have to come back."

He didn't know what that meant. Come back to what? To God? To Jocelyn? To the version of himself before all of this?

Before the lie? Before the city?

Gram's voice stayed with him, too. In dreams. In quiet moments. In the seconds right before he woke up and remembered who he was pretending to be that day. She was always gentle. Always kind. *"God's still here, sweetheart. Just talk to Him."* And sometimes, that voice in his head felt more real than anything else.

But he couldn't talk to God. Not honestly. Not now. Not after all he'd done. The women. The pills. The lies. The way he disappeared on Jocelyn again after getting her hopes up. The way he used Kristen's loneliness to cover his own. He told himself he'd come clean. That he'd find help. That he'd tell someone. But the days kept moving, and the silence kept growing, and he couldn't find the door back.

And so, he started writing again. Just little notes to himself. Scribbled lines on sticky notes or receipts. Truths he wanted to believe. Things Gram would've said. Things he used to tell Jacob. Things Jocelyn once whispered into his voicemail when he hadn't answered for weeks. *"You're still worth loving."* *"God doesn't keep score the way you think He does."* *"The shame isn't yours to carry."*

He never read them twice. Just wrote and folded them into his wallet or tucked them behind the mirror. But in some small way, they helped. For a minute. For a breath.

He left Kristen's apartment on Friday morning without waking her.

He told himself that leaving quietly was kindness. It was really rehearsal.

She was curled on her side, breathing heavily, a smear of

mascara still clinging to the edge of her cheek. He didn't know her last name. Couldn't remember how they'd met. And that terrified him.

His coat was slung across the back of a chair, half-draped in a stranger's black sweater. His shoes were still damp near the door. He dressed quickly, quietly. Stepped over discarded bottles. Avoided the broken glass by the bathroom door.

Outside, the city was too loud. Too clear. And his heartbeat too fast for the hour.

He took another Adderall. And then another.

His body said no. His calendar screamed yes. He obeyed the louder master.

Told himself it was for the spreadsheets. For the sales calls. For the brilliance they demanded. The math came quickly, but his thoughts didn't. His hands couldn't stop twitching, and his mouth was dry and hollow. No food. Just water. And the pills.

And when five o'clock came, he didn't stay late. He walked to Penn Station in a fog. His suit jacket clung to him like armor. He took a window seat on the quiet car, second row from the back, and leaned his head against the glass.

He typed, *On my way*, then stared at Jocelyn's name until the screen dimmed and went black. He didn't hit send.

The city pulled away like an apology he didn't believe anymore.

The hum of the tracks should've comforted him. It used to. But that night, everything felt foreign.

He tried to remember what it was like to be young. Before the hospital. Before the lie. Before the needing-to-be-perfect.

But all he could picture was Peter's face, blurry and fading. And Gram's voice, soft as ever, whispering the words she'd repeated to him since he was a boy:

You are loved. You are loved. You are loved.

But his body didn't believe it.

The pain started just after he stepped off the train.

A sharp heat spread across his chest, down his left arm. He tried to take a breath, but his lungs were stubborn. The cold night air punched at his ribs.

He made it halfway across the parking lot before his knees buckled.

A woman screamed.

A man shouted for help.

The pavement rushed to meet him.

The last thing he heard was the sound of someone dialing 911 and the faint crackle of the train pulling away behind him.

A single thought rose like a flare: *I'm not ready to die as this.* It didn't change what happened next.

And then—nothing.

When he woke, it was to a weight on his chest that wasn't physical. A stillness so dense it made the sterile air hum. His eyes blinked open to the blurred edge of fluorescent light overhead. He tried to move but couldn't—his wrists were strapped down at his sides, the IV line tugging slightly as his arm shifted. There was a tube still nestled in the corner of his mouth, taped in place, and he could taste plastic and salt. The hum of machines flickered in and out of his consciousness, and though his vision cleared slowly, it was the dread that came first. The shame. The dread. The sick, shattering recognition that he had survived.

There was a nurse. Someone charting his vitals, adjusting his line, whispering something professional but kind.

"You're okay," she murmured, more cadence than claim, as if the words themselves were part of the machinery keeping him there.

But he couldn't make out the words because everything inside him was screaming. He was still here. He was alive. And worse, someone might have seen him like this.

And then came Marie.

She entered quietly. No dramatic gasp, no rush to his side. Just that familiar controlled strength she'd always carried like armor. Her eyes were red but dry, her lips tight, her steps cautious. She stood beside him for a long moment before sitting, not looking at him, not yet.

"I almost didn't come," she said softly. "I didn't want to see you like this. But then I thought... maybe you didn't want me to see you like this either."

He swallowed. Or tried to. The tube kept him mute. She turned toward him now, finally facing him, and her expression softened—not into warmth, exactly, but into something tender. Something ancient.

"You were supposed to come see me. Remember? You said you were coming home. And then I got the call."

He tried to shape an apology with his eyes—*I meant to make it*—but the shame translated first.

He blinked hard, tried to answer with his eyes, tried to shape a word.

"I know," she said, her voice catching. "I know you didn't

mean for this. I know."

She reached for his hand and held it, tightly, her thumb brushing the back of his knuckles as if willing the blood to stay warm. It wasn't forgiveness. Not exactly. But it was love. And he didn't deserve it.

He wanted to close his eyes again and sleep for years. Disappear beneath the weight of it all and never have to remember how far he'd fallen.

But then Gram entered the room, and the silence lifted like smoke.

She didn't say anything at first. Just came to his side, her hand instinctively reaching up to stroke his hair like she did when he was small. She touched his forehead and then kissed it, her lips trembling against his skin. She took the chair on the other side of the bed, opposite Marie, and then pulled something from her bag—a little card. The kind she kept in her Bible. The kind she would send him in the mail sometimes when the distance between them grew too long to ignore.

She didn't show it to him. Just held it between her palms, folded as if in prayer.

"You're not gone, baby," she whispered. "You're still here."

"Breathe with me," Gram said, and matched his inhale like they were timing the ocean. For a moment, the room obeyed her.

His chest heaved with something unnamable. The tears fell sideways into the pillow. He felt six years old again. Felt the boy still buried under all the polish, all the striving, all the sin.

"Whatever happened," she said, leaning in so close her

breath warmed his cheek, "it doesn't get to have the last word."

She sat there for a long time, saying nothing more. And yet the silence between them said everything. He wanted to say he was sorry, but he couldn't move. So he let his eyes speak. Let the tears keep coming. Let the presence of her love begin to carve a path back to something that looked like grace.

Later, when the machines beeped lower and the room emptied for a moment, Jocelyn came in.

She looked like she hadn't slept in days. Her curls were wild, her eyes rimmed with exhaustion, and her posture stiff with resolve. She stood at the foot of the bed for a long moment, then stepped closer, her arms crossed tightly over her chest as if to keep herself from crumbling.

"I don't know what I expected," she said, voice tight. "But it wasn't this."

He blinked at her, desperate to explain, to give her some window into the war that led him here. But she shook her head before he could try.

"I'm not here to make you feel worse. I think you've got that covered."

"Safe isn't the same as alive," she added, softer now. "I want you alive."

She stepped closer, her eyes softening now, and for a moment she seemed to struggle between anger and tenderness. Between walking out and reaching for his hand.

"I never stopped loving you, Tristan. That's the problem. You broke every part of me that still wanted to believe you'd come back whole. And here you are, cracked wide open. Maybe this is what it takes."

She reached into the pocket of her jacket and pulled out a small folded note. Without another word, she slid it beneath his fingers and then turned to go.

He wanted to scream after her. To beg her to stay. But the words weren't ready. His voice was still locked inside the man he hadn't yet become. So he watched her walk away, watched the door swing closed behind her, and let the note burn in his hand like a second chance.

He didn't open it yet. Couldn't. Not until the room was silent again.

The silence felt familiar—the same hum, the same light, the same chair by the wall. The same waiting.

And then, sometime after the machines had settled and the nurses made their last rounds, the light in the room shifted.

There was a figure in the corner. A man. Familiar, somehow. Strong jaw, tired eyes. The kind of face that had once taught him how to tie a tie and then disappeared like smoke.

Peter.

But it couldn't be. Peter was gone. Gone long ago.

And yet he was there now, sitting calmly in the chair by the window, watching him with something like sorrow and something like peace.

"I never left, you know," Peter said.

Tristan blinked. His chest ached.

"I know you think it's your fault," Peter continued. "All of it. What happened. What you became.

But I let you go because I believed you'd come back."

Tristan tried to speak, but the words caught.

"You don't have to carry it anymore. The guilt. The fire. The lie. I see the boy inside you still trying to fix it. Still trying to earn what you already had."

I'm sorry, Tristan tried to say, the words crowding his throat until they were only heat.

Peter stood and stepped closer, reached down to touch Tristan's arm.

"You don't have to fix it. Just let it go."

And then he was gone. Not like he walked out. Just faded. Like a memory that had given its last gift.

The light changed again.

This time, it was a boy. Small. Luminous. He stood at the edge of the bed and looked at Tristan with a curiosity that bordered on knowing.

He didn't speak at first. Just stared. As if trying to decide what to say.

"I've been watching you," the boy finally whispered. "You're not who you're supposed to be."

Tristan's breath caught. There was something about the voice. The shape of the mouth. The light in his eyes.

"I think I'm going to have to do something about what you've become," the boy said, not unkindly. "I suppose I should start now."

"Breathe," the boy said, like an order wrapped in mercy. Tristan did, and the air didn't hurt as much.

And with that, he reached out and touched Tristan's chest, right where the pain lived. Right where the longing always stayed.

When the boy disappeared, the room felt heavy again. But it was a different weight now. Not shame. Not fear. Something like hope.

Tristan turned to the note Jocelyn had left and slowly unfolded it.

One line. Written in her unmistakable script.

I am your home. I've always known that. And so have you. Are you ready to come home?

The tears came hot and fast, and this time, he let them.

The waiting room was quiet again. Still. The lights above flickered slightly, and Tristan leaned back in his chair, eyes closed, hands trembling. He thought of Peter. Of the little boy. Of Gram's kiss on his forehead. Of Jocelyn's note. And for the first time since arriving, he didn't feel like running. He was ready. Or maybe just tired enough to stop hiding. He opened his eyes and looked down at his hands—open now, empty, waiting.

Chapter 9

THE RETURN

They used to say the darkest moments came just before the dawn. But that wasn't quite true. The dark was slow, steady, familiar—like breathing underwater. The real terror came with light. When your eyes adjusted. When your body remembered. When you realized you were still here. And there were witnesses.

In the waiting room, he pressed his forehead against the wall and closed his eyes.

The wall felt cooler than it should, as if whatever was on the other side was humming with life he couldn't quite place. He told himself it was the air vents. He didn't look up to check.

His arms wrapped tightly across his ribs like he was holding himself together. He whispered to no one, "I'm grateful I didn't die. I think." But it didn't feel like relief. It felt like exposure.

The Almost Tomorrow

The beeping had slowed, steadied. The nurses no longer hovered quite so close. The restraints had been loosened. But everything else remained. The shame. The humiliation. The sterile scent of his own undoing. His body had survived, but barely. His soul, though—it still felt like it was bleeding.

Marie came first. Her face wasn't composed or careful like the last time he saw her. She looked broken in ways he hadn't known she could be. Her hair pulled back in a crooked tie, eyes red-rimmed and heavy. She stood just inside the doorway for a long time before speaking, arms crossed tightly across her chest, like if she let them fall, she'd hit him.

For a second, he wondered if she'd been there longer than he'd realized—like she was waiting for him to wake from something, not just look at her.

"I didn't recognize you," she said finally, her voice cracked with betrayal and grief. "When I saw you collapsing in that parking lot... when they pulled you into the ambulance... I didn't even know who I was looking at."

He wanted to say her name. To say anything. But all he could do was turn his face toward her, a single tear falling sideways into the clean white pillow.

"We're twins," she whispered. "And I didn't know you. How does that happen?"

She sat beside him, eventually. Not touching him. Not yet. She looked around the room like it might give her answers. The IV, the monitors, the tangled wires and machines trying to keep his body regulated. Her voice lowered, softer now. "You just... disappeared, Tristan. From all of us. And I was so angry for so long. But then I saw you like this, and I didn't feel angry. I just felt like I'd already lost you."

The phrasing stuck—*already lost you*—as if she were

remembering something that hadn't happened yet.

That was when he broke. The dam opened. The tears came in hot silence, streaking sideways down his face while she sat beside him, still rigid but unmoving. After a few minutes, her fingers found his, laced through them loosely, like they'd once done under the table as children, waiting for their mother to stop yelling.

When she left, Gram came in.

There was no fanfare. Just the quiet creak of the door, the familiar scent of lavender and lemon balm, and the slight click of her shoes on tile. She didn't cry. She didn't scold. She just moved straight to his bedside and pulled the sheet up over his chest a little higher, her hands lingering near his heart.

"Well, you've made quite the mess of yourself, haven't you?" she said, her voice calm but unflinching.

His breath caught.

"And yet," she added, sitting beside him and clasping his wrist gently in both of her hands, "you're still mine."

That was all it took. The sobs came loud this time. Convulsing. Childlike. He didn't try to hold them back. Not with her. Not anymore.

She stayed with him all that night. Read scripture aloud when he dozed. Hummed old hymns when his heart rate climbed. Whispered stories from his childhood he thought he'd forgotten, stories of who he used to be. And when morning came, she announced that the doctors had cleared him for release, and that he would not, under any circumstances, be going back to that city.

"You're coming with me," she said. "To Florida. You're going to get clean. And you're going to remember who you are."

He didn't argue. He didn't have the strength to.

"I'll walk with you every step," she added, softening. "But there'll be no weaning off anything. No halfway healing. You're going to feel it, Tristan. All of it. And then you're going to get free."

The way she said it made him think she'd stood in this exact spot before, given these exact instructions. He couldn't place when.

Later that morning, Jocelyn arrived.

She was quieter than before. The note she had left him still rested in the pocket of his hospital gown. He hadn't shown anyone. Hadn't even told Gram about it. But he'd memorized the words. They lived in him now.

She didn't cry, either. She walked in like someone with a purpose, took one long look at him, and exhaled slowly.

"You look better than I expected," she said.

He smiled faintly, mouth dry. "You always did set the bar low."

That earned the faintest laugh. She took his hand, held it in both of hers.

"I talked to Marie. To Gram. I told them I'll stay close. However this goes."

He nodded.

"I'm not going to push you," she continued. "Not this time. But I need you to know—I still see you. Under all of it. The real you. And I'm not walking away."

He didn't have a reply. But when she bent down to kiss his forehead, he closed his eyes and let himself believe, if only for a moment, that maybe he was still someone worth loving.

They wheeled him out of the hospital before noon.

No one said discharge. No one brought paperwork. Just the motion of wheels and the sense that the hallway had no end until Gram's hand tightened around his.

No photographers. No fanfare. Just a broken man in a borrowed coat, headed for a detox he hadn't asked for but knew he needed. As they drove south, Tristan kept one hand in Gram's and the other gripping the note folded in his palm like scripture.

He didn't know what waited for him in Florida. Only that it would be hard. Only that it would be honest.

And maybe, finally, that it would be enough.

They arrived just after dark. The drive from Georgia was quiet, save for Gram's humming and the low, steady rhythm of rain against the windshield. Tristan watched the palm trees blur past like ghosts, their silhouettes barely visible in the wet glow of the headlights. Florida didn't feel like freedom yet. It felt like exile. Like judgment softened by sunshine. But Gram had packed the fridge, made the bed with clean linens, and lit a lavender candle before he even stepped foot inside. He stood in the doorway of the guest room—his room now—and exhaled for what felt like the first time in months.

The next morning began the way every morning would for the next three months: early. No pills. No coffee. No noise. Just Gram knocking softly on his door and saying, "Time to wake up, love. This is the day the Lord has made."

He hated it.

He hated the silence. The slowness. The way his body ached without the artificial sharpness of Adderall. The fatigue. The nausea. The hollow ringing in his ears that no music could drown. He shook at night. He snapped at her by day. Once, he even yelled. But Gram never flinched. Never matched his volume. She would just nod, sometimes sigh, and then begin reading Psalms aloud from the porch while he sat inside and stared blankly at the wall.

It took nearly two weeks for the haze to lift.

And when it did, he wept.

Not because he was healed, but because for the first time in years, he could feel the edge of something real again. Not performance. Not survival. Just presence.

Gram made tea every afternoon, steeped with lemon and ginger and love. She cooked breakfast whether he wanted it or not. She told stories from her childhood. About how she'd survived loss and silence and shame.

Some of them, he could swear, she'd never told him before. Others felt almost rehearsed, like she knew he'd need them again someday.

About how God had never once left her—even when she'd begged Him to. And Tristan, weak and hungry and hollow, started to believe that maybe the same could be true for him.

He slept more. Ate better. Read scriptures she left by his bedside and wrote things in a notebook he never showed her. The shakes disappeared. His skin regained color. His mind—once electric with overdrive—began to slow. Not into apathy. But into clarity.

Jocelyn called every day.

Sometimes in the morning. Sometimes at night. Sometimes twice. Their conversations weren't dramatic. She didn't ask for updates or status reports. She just talked. About her day. Her students. Her prayers. She shared poems she was reading and articles she found. He told her about the strange bugs in Florida and how Gram refused to let him leave the house until he'd journaled something honest.

One afternoon, he confessed to her that he still couldn't pray out loud. That it made him feel like a fraud.

"You don't have to speak to be heard," she said. "He already knows the parts you're afraid to say."

It silenced him in the best way.

By week four, he was running again. Just down the block and back. But it felt like flight. Like something in his lungs had remembered its purpose. By week six, he asked Gram if he could start writing music again, something he hadn't done since college. She just smiled, handed him her old guitar from the hall closet, and said, "Welcome back."

It wasn't just recovery. It was resurrection.

Still, the shame didn't leave.

Even clean, even surrounded by love, there were nights he lay in bed and stared at the ceiling, begging God to take the fire away. The one still burning in his chest. The one fueled by a lie he had never really forgiven himself for. He thought of Peter. Of the silence. Of the way the past still haunted him even after all these years.

And sometimes, in those long quiet hours, he still felt the presence of the boy.

The boy never seemed older. Never younger. Just fixed in the same faint glow, as if time couldn't touch him.

The one who glowed faintly. The one who didn't speak, not at first. The one who always appeared just as Tristan thought he might finally sleep. A boy who felt familiar in a way he couldn't explain—too small to be a stranger, too silent to be real.

He didn't run from him anymore. He just watched. And sometimes, in the flicker of candlelight across the wall, the boy would tilt his head slightly, like he saw something worth saving.

By the time October gave way to the colder hush of early November, the trees outside Gram's home had thinned, and the morning wind came with enough chill to make the windows rattle. He had gained back nearly twenty pounds. His face had softened, filled out again into the shape she recognized. His voice—once frayed at the edges—had steadied, as though the silence had stitched something back together. Most mornings, he still rose early, joined her on the back porch, and sipped her tea with one leg tucked beneath him like a boy learning to sit still again. But now he talked more. Laughed more. Sometimes he even prayed out loud.

He did not become someone else. That wasn't the point. What Gram had insisted on, and what he'd finally understood, was that recovery was not a rebranding. It was a return. A shedding of all the layers he had added in order to survive—a removal of costume, not character. He was not better because he had abstained. He was becoming whole because he had surrendered.

When he told her about the plans—that he and Jocelyn had been talking, more seriously now, about a life, a future, a home—Gram had nodded once, not with surprise but with the solemnity of someone who had seen it coming long before he did.

"I think she's always known," she said. "The question is—do you?"

He hadn't answered. Not at first. But that night, he had

written a letter. Not to Jocelyn. Not even to Peter. To himself. To the boy who still haunted his dreams. He didn't read it aloud. Just folded it neatly and left it between the pages of the Psalms.

His final days in Florida came with an odd stillness. No drama. No racing heart. Just a slow packing of bags and a tenderness in his chest that felt like gratitude sharpened by fear. Gram had booked his train ticket north. The plan was simple. He'd move to Pennsylvania, stay with a family friend—one of the pastors from Jocelyn's church—until the wedding.

The way Gram said it—like a certainty, not a plan—made him feel as though it had already happened and he was just catching up.

A few weeks at most. Jocelyn had offered to let him move in with her, but he'd declined. There was something sacred about waiting. About entering marriage from a place of calm, not convenience. And more than anything, he wanted to come to her whole.

He left just after Thanksgiving.

Gram didn't cry. She hugged him tightly, then pulled away and looked him square in the eyes.

"You've come back to life," she said. "Don't forget how you got here."

He kissed her cheek and whispered, "I won't."

Then he stepped into the car and didn't look back until the house disappeared from the rearview.

The train ride north was quiet, the tracks humming beneath him like a hymn. He spent most of the ride reading and watching the landscape shift from citrus groves to bare, frost-bitten hills. When he arrived, the pastor met him at the station, welcomed him with warmth and an awkwardness Tristan found oddly comforting. The house was small but full of life. Books on every shelf. Kids' shoes in the hallway. A dog that barked every time the wind changed direction. Tristan stayed in a spare room tucked behind the laundry room. He kept to himself mostly. Cooked when he could. Took long walks in the evening. Sent Jocelyn poems and prayers and half-written songs he still wasn't brave enough to sing.

Their conversations had changed, too. Not in tone, but in weight. She spoke about the venue. About flowers and music and vows. He listened, smiled, and offered thoughts when asked. But mostly, he just marveled at the fact that she still wanted him. That after all these years—all the silence and shame and almosts—she still saw something worth tethering herself to.

The days moved quickly. Fittings. Counseling sessions. Emails from out-of-town guests confirming their arrival. Jocelyn took care of most of it. Not because he wouldn't, but because she liked the details. The control. The order. Tristan found peace in that. He was learning, slowly, to let love look like something other than apology.

One night, two weeks before the wedding, she came over with dinner in a brown paper bag and sat cross-legged on the floor of his borrowed room.

"Do you believe in fate?" she asked between bites of salad.

He looked at her, thought for a moment, then shook his head.

"I believe in choice," he said. "In grace. In God putting people in our path over and over until we finally stop running."

She smiled at that. Didn't say anything. Just reached for his hand and held it there until the light in the hallway turned off.

The wedding was held in early January, on a bright, brittle day where the wind cut through coats but the sun refused to disappear. The sky had that sharp winter blue—endless and empty—and the trees stood bare like witnesses. The church was small, whitewashed, set off from the main road like it had been waiting for them all along.

Something in the stillness told him it might have been waiting longer than that.

Inside, the candles flickered against stained glass, and a warmth lingered despite the drafts that crept in under the doors. It was the kind of place where promises felt like they belonged.

Jocelyn's mother wept through most of the ceremony, and Gram sat near the front in a navy-blue coat with a corsage pinned over her heart, her eyes focused, her hands folded as if in silent prayer for every second of it. Tristan had arrived early, hours before anyone else, and stood alone in the sanctuary, eyes trailing along the wooden beams and worn pews, the sunlight that filtered through the colored panes. He could feel the weight of the moment pressing down like gravity—both beautiful and suffocating.

Stewart stood beside him, tall and strong, his tailored suit clinging to shoulders made wider by years of hard-earned success. His presence was grounding. The same boy who had once taught him how to throw a curveball, who'd driven him to rehearsals and sleepovers and talked about everything that didn't matter in order to say everything that did. Now he was finishing a fellowship in orthopedic surgery at Yale, engaged himself, wearing the same crooked half-smile that Tristan had memorized from middle school.

"You made it," Stewart said quietly as the guests settled in. "Didn't think you'd let anybody see the ending."

Tristan looked over at him, heart full, eyes already brimming. "It's not the ending," he said. "Not if I can help it."

When the music began, it was piano and strings—nothing dramatic, just delicate chords that rose and fell like breath. The back doors opened, and time slowed. She stood there in white.

Not the blinding, artificial white of magazines, but something soft, textured, almost glowing in the winter light. Her dress flowed like wind and grace, simple and perfect. Her hair was pinned back loosely, strands escaping to frame her face. And the smile—God, that smile—wasn't wide or performative. It was steady. Fierce. A knowing kind of joy. The kind you carry after you've bled for it.

Everyone stood. But all Tristan could do was stare.

Jocelyn walked down the aisle with her father at her side and never once looked away from him. Not when a toddler cried behind her. Not when the breeze caught the veil just so. Not when she passed the row where his mother sat, awkward and alone in a seat far enough from Gram to avoid tension, but close enough to be seen. She didn't flinch. Her eyes never left his.

He remembered what it felt like to see her for the first time in that AP English class. The way she'd called him out with a single glance. The way she knew him before he knew himself. And now, here she was, walking toward him like the answer to a question he hadn't known how to ask. When she reached him, she whispered just loud enough for him to hear, "Still breathing?"

He nodded, barely. She grinned.

The vows were simple. Honest. Neither of them tried to impress the crowd. They spoke to one another. She promised to see him. To fight for joy when it felt far off. He promised to tell the truth. To stay when everything inside him wanted to run. There were no elaborate metaphors. No poetic flourishes. Just tears. Laughter. And hands clasped so tightly it looked like they might never let go.

The reception was held in the church basement, transformed by Jocelyn's touch into something that resembled a winter fairy tale. White linen tablecloths, sprigs of cedar and eucalyptus tied with twine, candles in every corner. People clapped when they entered, raised glasses during the toasts, and wiped away tears when Gram stood to bless the meal.

There was a moment, just after the first dance, when Tristan stepped away from the noise. He walked slowly along the edge of the room, looking at faces—some familiar, some foreign. The Gallos had come. Jessica, too. Even Conor had flown in. His stepfather was seated alone near the back, nursing a soda and looking at Tristan like a man remembering something lost. His mother had spoken only briefly during dinner, congratulated Jocelyn, and excused herself early with a vague reference to a friend waiting in the car.

Tristan hadn't expected anything different.

He scanned the room again, just taking it all in, and that's when he saw him.

At a table near the wall, alone and slightly turned away, sat a man in a charcoal suit, hair thinning but eyes unmistakable. He wasn't speaking. Wasn't eating. Just watching. Calm. Present. Familiar.

Tristan's chest tightened. He walked toward the table slowly, each step weighed with disbelief.

"Peter?"

The man turned. Smiled gently. Said nothing. Tristan's breath caught. He knelt slightly beside the table, not caring how odd it looked. He didn't touch him. Just stared.

"I didn't think you'd come," he said, his voice barely audible above the music.

Peter's expression didn't change. "I've never really been gone."

The words landed heavy, not just as comfort but as if they applied to more than Peter—as if none of this had really left him.

Before Tristan could respond, Jocelyn appeared at his side. "There you are," she said softly.

"Come on. People want pictures."

He stood, heart pounding, and gestured toward the table. "I want you to meet—"

But the chair was empty.

Just a folded napkin and an untouched plate of cake.

Jocelyn touched his arm gently, not surprised, not confused. Just deeply, heartbreakingly kind.

"I know you really wanted him to come," she said. "I'm so sorry, sweetie."

He didn't speak. Just nodded and let her lead him back into the swirl of music and congratulations and the smell of cinnamon and coffee and candle wax.

They hadn't called his name yet. He had checked the clock four times in the last ten minutes and still couldn't remember what time he got there. The air was thick with antiseptic and silence. The kind of silence that settled between ribs, that wrapped itself around the edges of your breathing and whispered,

"You're not safe yet."

He was alone again. The nurse had come and gone. The other two people in the room were staring at their phones, quiet and disconnected, strangers wrapped in their own invisible storms. The television on the wall flickered with muted news coverage, subtitles rolling beneath a panel of talking heads who looked far too polished to be trusted.

Tristan sat forward slightly, elbows on knees, hands clenched together, head bowed. He wasn't praying. He didn't know how to pray for this. But he was remembering. And the remembering was a kind of penance.

He had thought the wedding was the turning point.

But sometimes, in the quieter spaces since, he wondered if it had been more like a story he'd been allowed to step into for a while. A quiet reprieve for his mind.

That beautiful cold January day, Jocelyn's hand in his, the scent of cedar and white roses clinging to her dress, Gram beaming from the second row. It had felt like something had finally stitched closed. Like all of it—the lie, the fire, the shame—had been forgiven just by showing up, by making it to that altar. He had been so sure.

But three years had passed. And in that space, something had cracked again.

It wasn't dramatic. That's what scared him most. There was no single moment, no betrayal, no sharp turning point. Just slow ambition. Just busyness. A new job. A second promotion. Late nights, early flights, calls he didn't take, texts he meant to answer. Jocelyn had said, gently at first, that she missed him. That she missed *them*. That they hadn't prayed together in weeks. That he wasn't sleeping. That he wasn't really there when he was home.

And he told her he was tired. That he was doing it for them. That this season would pass.

But seasons stretch when no one's counting the days. And somewhere between the boardroom and the status updates, between the expectations of everyone who once whispered "gifted" and the pressure of finally being seen as successful, he lost the very thing that had brought him back to life.

He lost himself.

And now he didn't know if it was too late.

Gram hadn't said much when he called a week ago and told her things were bad again. That Jocelyn had left to stay with a friend. That she had said, through tears, that she loved him but didn't know how to love *this version* of him. Gram hadn't said, "I told you so." She had only asked if he still believed he was loved.

He couldn't answer.

In the waiting room, he shifted. Rested his forehead against his clenched hands. The quiet was too loud. The memories too close. He wanted to run. To scream. To break something. To take back every meeting he said yes to, every client he chose over dinner, every moment Jocelyn asked him to slow down and he said he couldn't. Every glance in the mirror where he saw the fire behind his eyes and told himself it was ambition, not fear.

Because now, sitting here, he wasn't sure if she'd come back.

He could still feel her note folded in his pocket. The one she gave him in the hospital three years earlier, the one he hadn't dared to reread since. He carried it everywhere. Like a talisman.

Like proof.

But paper is fragile. And promises, even the sacred ones, can tear. He closed his eyes and whispered it again. The prayer that wasn't quite a prayer. "Please. Just... please." He was no longer sure who he was talking to. God. Jocelyn. Gram. Himself.

The door opened and a nurse stepped halfway into the room. She called a name that wasn't his, and he flinched anyway. His heart raced in anticipation of something he wasn't sure he deserved.

Something that had always felt too good to hold onto.

He imagined her not showing up. Imagined getting in the car alone. Driving back to a house that no longer felt like home. Imagined sleeping on her side of the bed because it was the only place that still smelled like grace.

And he imagined something worse.

That this room had always been the constant, and everything else had only ever been a visit.

That maybe love wasn't enough this time. That maybe he had finally run out of chances.

"I'm grateful I can still feel," he whispered into the hush, though this time the words sounded less like thanks and more like a confession.

Because if this was the end...

If Jocelyn was already gone...

If this was the last time he'd sit in a place hoping to be called, hoping to be chosen...

Then the waiting room wasn't just a space anymore.

It was the judgment.

And he wasn't sure he could survive it.

Chapter 10

THE COUNSELOR

The room hadn't changed.

He was still in the hospital, tethered to the quiet machinery of survival. Somewhere beyond the edges of this stillness, a monitor ticked his pulse, and a slow drip of fluid pressed its way into his veins. His chest rose and fell with the effort of a body remembering how to live. The weight of the overdose was leaving him—sweated out, purged in the silent work of his organs—but his mind was somewhere else entirely, wide open and raw.

This space—this unfolding—was as real as the cold metal railing against his wrist. As real as the dull ache in his ribs, the sting in the crook of his arm, the hollow hunger in his gut. Sometimes, when the body reaches the brink and the mind finally shatters, a door opens. A place where the soul can speak what it has held for a lifetime.

The chairs were the same. The light still hummed with that faint, sterile buzz. But something in Tristan had shifted.

He was no longer pacing. No longer glancing at the exit every few seconds, calculating his escape. He just sat there, hands resting on his knees, his eyes low. He didn't know if he had been there minutes or hours or days. Time had started to lose its grip on him, peeling away in slow flakes like paint from an old wall.

Then she came in.

Gram.

Not as a memory. Not as a dream. Not as a flicker of conscience. But whole. Present. Dressed in the soft green sweater she always wore when the weather turned. She moved toward him like the air itself made room for her.

Tristan stood—he couldn't help it—and he almost buckled. But Gram reached out and held him steady, both hands on his arms, like she had done when he was six and shattered and she'd bent low to lift him off the cold floor.

"You look tired, baby," she said, her voice a low hush, as if she'd come to tuck him in one last time.

"I don't want to be here," he said. His voice cracked, half-boy, half-man. "Not like this."

"I know," she said. "But sometimes the best beginnings feel a lot like endings."

He didn't speak.

Gram walked him to the bench again, and they sat. Shoulder to shoulder. Like they used to on her porch, listening to cicadas and drinking ginger ale out of glass bottles.

"I thought I was better," he whispered. "I thought I fixed it. I was with Jocelyn. I was clean. I felt..." He trailed off. "I thought we had more time."

"You did get better," she said, without correcting him. "And you'll get better again. Love isn't a destination, sweetheart. It's a rhythm. Sometimes we fall out of step. But the music doesn't stop just because we lose the beat."

"I told her I'd change."

"And you meant it," Gram said gently. "That matters."

He turned to her, eyes stinging. "She's everything I wanted."

"I know," Gram said. "But you have to want yourself, too. You've spent so long trying to be someone who could be loved that you forgot—you already were."

Tristan wiped his face with the heel of his hand. "I don't know how to do this. I don't know where to start."

"Start with breath," she said. "Start with truth. Start with the boy."

He stilled. "The boy?"

She looked toward the corner, and when Tristan followed her gaze, he saw him—barely. Just a shimmer at first. A silhouette. The outline of a child bathed in a faint light, standing with hands folded in front of him. Watching. Waiting.

Gram didn't explain.

She didn't have to.

Instead, she took Tristan's hand and placed something inside it. A small, warm coin. No markings. Just weight. Presence.

"What is it?" he asked.

"A reminder," she said. "That you still carry something whole inside you."

He looked down, then back up—but she was already standing.

"Where are you going?"

"I've been here," she said with a soft smile. "Now it's time for someone else."

"Gram..."

She leaned down and kissed his forehead. "You're not alone, Tristan. Not now. Not ever."

And then she was gone.

Just like that.

He closed his hand around the coin and looked toward the boy again—but the boy hadn't moved. Still standing there, far enough away to remain more symbol than person. And behind him, from the far edge of the room, came the sound of approaching footsteps.

He turned.

Peter.

Not the angry man, not the ghost of a past soaked in shame—but the soft-eyed figure he remembered from the stories Gram used to tell. Before it all went wrong. Before the fire.

Peter didn't speak at first. He just nodded, the way men do when they've both survived something neither of them knows how to name.

Then he held out a hand.

Tristan rose.

And they walked toward the boy, not yet close enough to reach him.

But closer than before.

The room held its breath as Peter stepped into view.

Tristan froze where he stood. His chest tightened, his hands slack at his sides, and for a moment he could only stare, as if the man before him might vanish if he blinked. Peter's presence was not loud or commanding—it was soft, almost hesitant. He wasn't the ghost of nightmares or the shadow that haunted the edges of Tristan's memory. He was just... a man. Older than he remembered, but somehow lighter.

"Peter..." The name fell from his lips like a confession.

Peter tilted his head, his eyes scanning Tristan slowly, as if memorizing him. "You look older," he said finally, his voice low but even. "Tired... but older."

Tristan's throat closed around the thousand things he wanted to say. He tried to hold himself still, but the weight of it all—years of shame, guilt, silence—began to crush him. His knees buckled, and he sank to the floor, sobs breaking free before he could stop them.

"I'm sorry," he whispered, then louder, "I'm so sorry."

The words spilled like water from a burst dam. He clutched at his face, fingers trembling, rocking forward as if the motion might release the ache inside him. He couldn't meet Peter's eyes, not yet. "I knew. Even as a kid, I knew it wasn't true. I knew I was lying. I let her... I let Elizabeth... I let her spin it. I let her say it louder so I wouldn't have to." He shook his head violently. "And I let it ruin you."

Peter walked closer, slow and measured, then knelt down until they were eye to eye. He didn't reach for him. He didn't touch him. He just waited until Tristan could look up.

"You were a boy," Peter said softly.

"I knew better," Tristan said through ragged sobs. "I knew better, and I still said it. I let them believe it. I let the fire take everything from you, and I hid behind it like a coward. I let myself live, and I let you... disappear."

Peter studied him for a long, quiet moment. "You think that one lie was all of me?"

Tristan blinked, confused.

Peter's gaze softened, and a strange, almost wistful smile curved his mouth. "I was already halfway gone before that. I didn't know how to stay. I didn't know how to be what anyone needed. Not your mother. Not you. Not myself." He looked down, exhaling slowly. "The lie hurt. It carved something out of me. But it didn't create the emptiness. It just showed me where it was."

Tristan's chest hitched. "I wanted you to come back."

"I know."

"I wanted you to fix it. To… to make it all okay. Even after I lied. Even after you were gone."

"I know." Peter's voice was steady, not unkind. "But I couldn't. I didn't know how. And by the time I wanted to try… it was too late for me to do it the way you needed."

Tristan dropped his head into his hands again. His voice cracked when he said, "I ruined you."

Peter shook his head slowly. "No, son. Life broke me long before that. You were just a boy trying to survive." He paused, then added with quiet gravity, "I wish I'd been the kind of man who could see that sooner."

Somewhere behind the vision, a monitor beeped softly, reminding him his body was still here, clinging to life while his soul did its work.

The silence that followed was heavy but alive, the kind that fills a room with more than absence.

Tristan's breathing slowed. He wiped his face with trembling hands. "I saw you in every fire after that," he whispered. "Every shadow. Every night. I blamed myself. I hated myself. I thought if I could build a perfect life, maybe... maybe I could undo it."

Peter's gaze drifted to the far corner of the room. Tristan followed his eyes—and there, still and silent, stood the boy. The faint light around him made the floor look like water, as though he were standing on the reflection of some better world.

"I thought he was yours," Peter said quietly.

Tristan frowned through the blur of tears. "The boy?"

Peter nodded. "The first time I saw him... he didn't speak. He just sat by me. Weeks, maybe months. I couldn't tell anymore. I thought I was imagining him. Thought maybe my mind was slipping. But he kept coming back." His voice thickened. "And little by little... I started to believe he wasn't here to haunt me. He was here to show me I wasn't gone. Not really."

Tristan stared at the boy, a fresh ache blooming in his chest.

"He came to you, too," Peter continued. "Because he isn't just yours. He's ours. He's... everybody's, I think. If they'll see him. If they'll let themselves."

Something in Tristan broke open at those words—a crack deep in the foundation of the shame he had carried all his life. His voice trembled. "He loved you, too?"

Peter's smile was faint but real. "He did. He does. He made me believe in something I never really understood. I didn't have faith the way your Gram did. I didn't pray. I didn't know how to. But sitting with him felt like... being forgiven without anyone saying the words. Like being a boy again. Like having one more chance to see the world without all the dirt on it."

Tristan let the tears come again. They were quieter this time, cleaner somehow. "I wanted to give that to you," he said. "All those years. I wanted you to feel what I felt when I first saw him. I wanted to tell you I was sorry, and that I loved you, and that I missed you."

"You just did," Peter said gently.

Tristan's lips trembled. He glanced at the boy, then back to Peter. "I wish I could go back."

"You can't." Peter reached out now, finally, and placed a hand on Tristan's shoulder. Warm. Steady. "None of us can. But you can go forward. And you can carry him with you. That's enough."

For a long time, neither spoke. Tristan felt the weight of Peter's hand, the truth of his words, and the quiet presence of the boy watching.

"Do you forgive me?" Tristan whispered.

Peter hesitated. Then he shook his head—not in rejection, but in a deeper truth. "I don't need to. It's already gone. You've been holding ashes, son. There's no fire left to burn you."

Tristan broke, but this time it wasn't the shattering of guilt. It was release. He leaned forward, and Peter pulled him into an embrace that was neither desperate nor hesitant. It was simple. Human. Two lives acknowledging what was lost, and what still remained.

When they finally parted, Peter studied him one last time. "You need to follow him now," he said, nodding toward the boy. "He's waiting for you."

Tristan nodded, wiping his face.

Peter rose slowly. He took a step back, his eyes warm, his presence already lighter. "I'm at peace, Tristan. I need you to be, too."

Tristan wanted to speak, but the words caught in his throat. He only managed a soft, "Thank you."

Peter smiled, small and sure. "You were always more than your worst moment."

And then he was gone. Not abruptly, not like a ghost vanishing—but like dusk fading into evening. The space he'd occupied still felt alive, full of warmth, but empty of weight.

Tristan turned to the boy, still glowing in the corner. For the first time, he felt ready to take a step toward him.

The room felt different now.

Not emptier—quieter. The kind of quiet that comes after a storm, when the rain has soaked through everything and the world is still deciding what to do with the water.

Tristan sat on the edge of the hospital bed, hands limp in his lap, chest still raw from the hours that had bled into this moment. Peter was gone. Gram had gone. Jocelyn, too. All that was left was the soft rhythm of the monitor and the boy, standing in the corner like a sentinel made of light.

For the first time, Tristan didn't look away. He couldn't.

The boy wasn't smiling. He wasn't frowning either. His expression held something that made Tristan's throat tighten—patience, maybe. Or knowing. Or the kind of love that doesn't rush.

And it broke something open in him.

"You," Tristan whispered, his voice splintering. "Where were you?"

The boy didn't move.

Tristan's voice rose, words tumbling fast now, the way they used to when he was a child trying to explain something no one would believe. "Where were you when I was six years old, sitting on that cold floor with my hands over my ears because the fire alarm wouldn't stop screaming? Where were you when they strapped me to that hospital bed because I wouldn't stop asking questions, because I was too curious, too loud, too alive?"

He shook his head, hands clenching. "You weren't there. You weren't. I looked for you. I begged for you. Gram told me there was a God who watched little boys, who kept them safe. She said if I prayed, someone would hear. But no one came. You didn't come."

The boy tilted his head slightly, listening. Still silent.

Tristan's chest tightened. He felt heat rise in his face, not from shame this time, but from the wild edge of grief. "Where were you when Peter left? When Elizabeth told me what to say? When I let the words out of my mouth and felt my whole life crack under the weight of them? I was just a boy! I didn't understand. And when I finally did, it was too late. Everything was already on fire—inside and out—and you were nowhere!"

His voice cracked on the last word. He pressed the heels of his hands to his eyes, hard, until the bright stars came, but it didn't stop the tears. He bent forward, his shoulders shaking.

"You let me keep that lie," he said hoarsely. "You let me carry it. Through every grade, every house, every night I stared at the ceiling and begged not to wake up. Where were you when I lost myself in all those lies I told just to keep people from seeing how broken I was? Where were you when I drowned it all in pills and Adderall and one-night stands and fake smiles and—"

He choked off the words, breath hitching, the sob rising through him like it had been trapped in his bones for decades.

The boy didn't move.

Tristan drew in a jagged breath, head shaking. "Do you even know how many times I begged for you? How many times I thought if I could just see you—just once—maybe I wouldn't feel like I was disappearing?" He lifted his head, his tear-streaked face raw and open. "And then you show up now? After everything? After Peter's gone, after I've burned my life down to ashes, after I lay face-down on the cold concrete of that train station—vision blurring, cheek against the floor, the taste of metal and dirt in my mouth—my body convulsing as the lights exploded and vanished, only to wake up strapped to a hospital bed, pain everywhere, light everywhere? Where were you then?"

His voice broke on the last word. It echoed off the walls and came back smaller, as if the room itself grieved with him.

He buried his face in his hands, rocking slightly. "I needed you," he whispered. "I needed you when I was small and scared and nobody believed me. I needed you when I watched everything I loved go up in smoke. I needed you when they sent me away, when they told me I was broken, when the only thing I could hear was my own heartbeat begging me to be good enough to stay alive. I needed you."

His words fell into the room like stones into deep water. No splash. Just weight.

The boy didn't speak. Didn't move.

So Tristan kept going.

"I needed you when they called me a liar. When they looked at me like I was something that needed to be fixed. When the world felt like it was made of fire and cold steel and the only soft place I knew was Gram's arms. I needed you when I got older, when I started to think maybe I could outrun it, maybe if

I just became perfect enough, no one would see the ashes I was carrying inside. I needed you when I got to college and thought maybe I could finally belong, but I was still that scared little boy pretending to be someone he wasn't. I needed you when Jocelyn looked at me with those eyes that said she saw me, and I couldn't let her, because I was afraid she'd see what I really was."

Tears burned down his cheeks again. He felt wrung out, hollowed by the memories pouring through him. "I needed you when I left for the city and thought maybe money and lights and being wanted would make me whole. I needed you on the nights I was too high to know my own name. I needed you when I woke up in beds that weren't mine, in apartments that smelled like smoke and strangers, and I stared at the ceiling and begged for the boy I used to be to come back and tell me I hadn't ruined everything."

His voice broke again, but he didn't stop.

"I needed you when I got on that train to see my sister. I needed you when my chest felt tight and my hands shook and I told myself I could keep it together, that I could hold all of it in for just a few more hours. I needed you when I felt my legs give out and the world tilt, and I tasted dirt and metal and blood and thought, 'This is it. This is how I leave.'"

The words trembled into a whisper. "Where were you?"

The boy's expression was the same—steady, patient, unshaken.

Tristan slumped forward, elbows on his knees, head in his hands. His sobs came quieter now, like something deep inside had cracked and the grief was spilling free, slow and inevitable. The room smelled of antiseptic and memory, sharp and clean. He could hear the distant hum of life beyond the door—nurses, machines, a world that kept moving while he unraveled in this stillness.

Minutes passed. Maybe more. He didn't know. All he knew was the release of finally saying what had lived like a knot in his chest for years. He had screamed and whispered and begged and accused, and still, the boy didn't leave.

Finally, his voice rasped out one last question, barely audible: "Why did it take losing everything for you to come?"

And the room went quiet again, waiting.

The room had gone so quiet, Tristan could hear the faint click of the IV drip behind him, the whisper of air as the machine breathed with him. His tears had slowed to a quiet ache. His chest felt raw, emptied by the weight of all he had said. And still, the boy had not moved.

Then, finally, the boy spoke.

"Tristan," he said, his voice soft and even, carrying like a note in a cathedral, filling every corner of the room. "I needed two things from you."

Tristan's head lifted. He didn't breathe.

The boy took a slow step forward, the light around him catching the edge of the bed. "First, I needed you to break all the way to the bottom. Not the kind of breaking that comes and goes with bad nights and regrets. The kind that reaches the last floor of your soul. The place where all the noise stops, and all the masks fall, and you have nothing left to hold but the truth."

He took another step, voice steady, patient.

"And then," the boy said, "I needed you to wait a little longer. To stay there. To find your true bottom. Because I knew you. I knew every part of you—the gift in your mind, the fire in your heart, the quiet ache for goodness you carried even when you couldn't speak it. I knew that you would hold on with every fiber of your life, long past the point most people would let go, until there was nothing left to break. Nothing left to protect. Nothing left to hide behind."

Tristan's lips trembled.

The boy's gaze was unwavering. "Because I knew that after all of that... you would be ready to see me."

The words hung in the air, soft and heavy, and something in Tristan's chest loosened like a knot undone after years of pulling tight. His shoulders sagged. His breath shook.

"I don't understand," he whispered.

The boy nodded. "You've spent your whole life trying to earn what was already yours. You wore the lie like a coat you couldn't take off. You thought if you could be perfect enough— if you could build the right life, chase the right dreams, hide the right pain—you could make the world forget what you thought you'd ruined."

Tears welled in Tristan's eyes again. "I thought I had to carry it. All of it. Forever."

"I know," the boy said. "But I was carrying you. Even then."

Tristan shook his head. "Then why didn't you come? Why didn't you stop the fire? The hospital? The nights I prayed and nothing happened?"

The boy took another step closer. He was close enough now that Tristan could see the light in his eyes—a reflection of his own. "Because my work wasn't to stop the world. It was to keep you whole inside it. I was in the quiet reaches of your heart, healing the little wounds as they came, even when more came after. I knew the shape of your heart when it was whole, Tristan. I held onto that shape when you couldn't. I knew this day would come."

Tristan's chest hitched. His voice was a whisper. "I thought I was alone."

"You were never alone," the boy said simply. "You were just waiting to be ready to believe it."

Something in Tristan cracked again, but this time it wasn't the jagged break of grief—it was release. Warmth spread through his chest like sunlight through open windows.

"You were always forgiven here," the boy continued, tapping a small hand against his own chest. "It was yourself you couldn't forgive."

The words sank into Tristan like water into dry soil. He covered his face with his hands and let the tears come again, softer now, each one a drop of something leaving him for good.

When he could finally speak, his voice was hoarse. "But what about her?"

The boy tilted his head. "Elizabeth?"

Tristan nodded, jaw tight. "She… she's the reason all of this happened. She told me what to say. She let the lie grow. She destroyed everything. I lost my childhood because of her. I lost Peter. I lost myself."

His voice rose, breaking again as years of buried anger bled through. "How could I ever forgive that? How could I forgive the fire, the nights in that hospital, the years of pretending I wasn't dying inside, the ache that never went away? How do you forgive the person who handed you the first stone in the avalanche that buried your life?"

He shook his head violently, hands gripping the sheets. "I can't. I can't. I don't know how to let that go."

The boy listened without flinching, his small face soft with understanding. He let the silence hold for a long moment before he spoke.

"Tristan," he said gently, "forgiving her doesn't make what happened right. It makes you free."

Tristan swallowed hard, his throat aching.

The boy stepped closer and lowered his voice, like he was telling a secret meant only for Tristan. "I may not be the only child here for you. The woman you remember was once a perfect child, too. There is a little girl here for her—waiting to guide her home, to show her the way back to the light she forgot."

Tristan's eyes lifted slowly, following the boy's gaze to the far corner of the room. There, faint as mist in morning sun, stood a small glowing girl. She was still and silent, her face unreadable, but her presence filled the air with something soft and unspoken.

Tristan's breath caught. "Who is she?"

The boy smiled faintly. "She is what waits for you to continue your journey."

"I don't understand," Tristan whispered.

"Now that you've forgiven yourself," the boy said, "it's time to forgive others. Only then will your heart be free enough to do what it was created to do. Forgiving yourself is the first step. Forgiving the ones who hurt you most… that's where your true gift begins to grow. That is where you become whole enough to change the world around you."

The words washed over Tristan like light breaking through water. He looked back at the little girl, and something inside him shifted—an understanding that was less about logic and more about release.

The boy reached out his hand. Tristan hesitated, then took it. Warmth, steady and grounding, spread through him like a quiet fire.

"You are whole now," the boy said. "Not because nothing happened, but because everything that mattered is still here."

Tristan closed his eyes, inhaled deeply, and for the first time in his life, the breath didn't feel like a battle. It felt like a beginning.

He opened his eyes, and the room seemed different. Softer. Luminous. The boy's hand was still in his, and in the far corner, the little girl waited, patient and silent.

Tristan rose slowly from the bed, unsteady but lighter than he had ever been. His body still ached, but the weight inside him was gone. He turned to the boy, his voice steady, quiet.

"What now?"

The boy smiled, small and sure. "Now, you begin again."

As Tristan took a step toward the glowing frame, he felt the weight of years slide from his shoulders like an old coat. He imagined Gram's porch, Jocelyn's eyes, Peter's quiet nod—and for the first time, he felt worthy of all of it.

Proud. Whole. New.

The boy didn't lead. He walked beside him.

And Tristan understood that this door wasn't only his. Somewhere, in every life, a door like this waits to be opened.

And when they reached the door, glowing softly at the edges, Tristan did not hesitate.

He opened it.

EPILOGUE

As the lights in the hospital room flicker softly, Tristan stirs once again. His body is weary, but the fragments of a truth he's long denied begin to settle in his chest. The journey is far from over. What he's learned in these moments of darkness and light is only the beginning, and the path ahead is still tangled with the scars of his past and the weight of forgiveness he has yet to embrace fully.

But the walls of his heart, once barricaded against love and healing, have cracked open just enough to let in a sliver of grace. Tristan knows now that the safe place he's been searching for wasn't a place at all. It's something he must create—within himself, with those he holds dear, and through the healing power of faith.

As he looks toward the future, there's a quiet certainty in his heart that his journey is not yet complete. The man he was, broken and lost, is still there—but something new is beginning to take shape.

What comes next will demand all that he has—his courage, his willingness to face his own truths, and his ability to surrender fully to the love and grace that have always been there, waiting.

The road to redemption is never straight, but Tristan is ready to walk it.

And so, the next chapter of his story begins.

www.ingramcontent.com/pod-product-compliance
Lightning Source LLC
Chambersburg PA
CBHW060418260626
47161CB00005B/1687